Disclaimer: This is a work of fiction. Any resemblance of actual places and persons is coincidental, outside of verifiable fact.
© 2022 Armanis Ar-feinial
All rights Reserved.
Edited by Aimee Hill
ISBN 979-8-9861041-4-0

Also by Armanis Ar-feinial

<u>The Fallen</u>
The Secrets of Terra Silenti
The Covenant
The Desecration of the World

<u>The Holy Grail War</u>
The Hedgehog
The Nihilistic Neverending Nightmare

Lira

To Tedward

Author's Introduction

It brings me great felicity in no small account, that you should happen to find yourself flipping through these pages, or on your device to read this book. I hope it brings some form of satisfaction upon your soul, hungry for words, hungry for the characters, and a sense of adventure that can only be achieved through the written word, and as you might tell, potentially already slouched over with a weakness about your shoulders, or wearily keeping your eyelids open all the while reading this rather long sentence; a significant influence came from Jane Austen, a much better wordsmith than I will ever be. But one could dare trust to hope just a little that her words and elegant flowery, but tight prose would make it in some form of the story, in which, you are about to read, just a semblance of her spirit may impart upon us all. Should this resonate with you in some way, I implore you to leave a review, whether for good or ill, or something in between.

To my Dear Tedward,

It's been a while since we've parted ways. How sorry I am that I haven't had the time to write to you until now, things have been crazy moving around, but fortunately John Spadero, you remember him don't you? He found us places to live and work, all relatively close to one another. He's a fine person once you get to know him for who and what he truly is. He's a bit rough around the edges. Kind of like you. Somedays I look at him, and I see you. I look up into the stars at night, and wonder where exactly they've got you shipped, or doing God only knows what, and for what purpose. I'm working in a lab, just like I used to, studying mutating germs and bacterium, as I used to.

Regrettably, I never spoke too much time about work, but I don't think you want to talk about researching bacterium. Boring to talk about, exciting to watch, almost like taking a deeper look into the footprint of creation, the world God intended us to live in, but not the one that we got. The world we got is far from perfect, not ideal, dirty, black, and grey filled with so much discourse it can drive you insane. It can be the cause for creating jobs, like yours, that should not exist.

Tedward, my poor dear Tedward.

I pray for you every night you know. I went to bed after star gazing. I pray for your health, your physical and mental health. Both, I know can't be all that great, but you know that. No one knows better than you. I know more than everyone else, sure, but still. I know it doesn't mean a whole lot right now, but that's all I can really do when you're wherever you are, and I'm here.

We never did spend much time star gazing. Too much light pollution, terribly dreadful business. I didn't know you for exceptionally long, but there are so many things I would have wanted to do with you. I know now that the list of what you could manage was entirely limited. And I know that you *wouldn't* have gone through that had you known it was going to trigger you. I mean that little concert that we went to. It's surreal to keep thinking this, but I can't help but mention it, there are days where I wonder if you're still alive, since those four people took you away from me, from us.

I know Sam, Michael, and Tim aren't asking about you right now. Too busy getting settled in with their new jobs. Oh! You didn't know this, but Michael proposed to Samantha, the other day and she said yes. Well, neither of them was ever the romantic type. Never read Jane Austen for personal enjoyment. I remember our little swapping of Jane Austen characters when you picked me up from the hospital that day. Do you remember? I remember. The Chariot. The Chariot awaits! Oh, I loved that. I wish I could have that again, the thrill of adventure, the wind in my hair as you push me right through the parking lot and opened the door for me like a little lady.

Now that I dwell on it, I think I vaguely remember seeing the Ilya who took you. The one that, more than anything else, knew pain. Spadero knew it too. I see it in his eyes, the same pain in your eyes. It hurts me still. I can see it when I pray for you. Again, I know it isn't much, but still. I'll try to write to you weekly. I know it probably takes two weeks to get to you, or perhaps longer, but I'd like to keep a rhythm going.

What's it been now? About two months since we've seen each other. I think that's accurate. I want you to know, I still have that necklace you bought me for Christmas. I can now reasonably say, since everything in my apartment was destroyed during the siege, that this necklace, which has your scent on it, that has your sweat on it, that has your heart on it, is the most prized physical thing I now possess. And when I see it, I think of you.

I miss you Tedward. Please, if it is within your power, please write back to me, will you? I'd love to hear something. A call, a letter, or, if you decide to write a letter, I want to see your handwriting!

I'm going to tell you something. I want it to be known so there may be a record of it on your heart, and I'm sure you suspected it all along. But what I'm about to tell you I'm certain you've heard it expressed to you often in life, and I'm abundantly aware, and concerned that you don't hear these words too often. Words are supposed to mean something and shouldn't be tossed around so lightly as I appear to be scribbling all over this page.

I know you feel the same way. Otherwise, I doubt I would even have such a precious gift from you.

I love you.

Well, that's embarrassing but I mean it, and I know you mean it too. I look forward to hearing from you. I will write weekly whether you write back to me or not. Once a week. That's not too pushy, is it? Well, I'd say it's just on brand!

~Jennifer

My dearest Tedward,

I know I know you likely didn't get the last letter yet. Probably still sitting alone in its own little box at the post office before it reached royal Britain. Alone. That's how you were when you found us. No. It would be no mistake to say that God placed you in front of us, and an opportunity, though seemed forced, we didn't miss it. And we weren't meant to miss you there, Tedward. That was no mistake. None of it. Everything that happened is the way God ordained it.

I know you came to Church with me on Sundays, and continued with those studies with me on Tuesdays, but I suppose I never did ask. I was always so concerned for you, we all were, and while there have been layers slowly stripped away revealing to us your true nature, though your identity remained secret (we know why now, and we don't fault you for it). I must ask though, since John S. will never tell us anything about your whereabouts or what have you, do you believe in God? Did you try? Perhaps you'll find some solace that He is good.

I say that now, but everything you've gone through has shown you quite the contrary. How can God be good when he took you from your parents? How can God be good when He allowed you to be used as a tool and abandoned? How can God be good when He allowed your friends to die in front of you? How can He be so Good when you're branded a traitor? How can He be good when He gave you into their hands, and they did horrible, despicable things to you? How can God be good when you watch the world you helped create, help it experience what true peace was, to watch it shatter almost overnight?

When I think about you, I think about these questions. I try to put myself in your shoes, and while some of it I can relate to, half of everything I can't begin to imagine even in my worst nightmares. My worst! Nightmares, Tedward. I look at these things, and see the horrors in your mind, and even now, I still see the flames, the blood from those weeks, I hear the gunfire in my sleep, and the soundless screams. They will never, never equate to what you've been through. For you've been through so much worse.

May the Lord deal with me ever so severely should the words I speak not be true. But I'm sorry. I'm sorry that your innocence was lost. I'm sorry that your friends and comrades were murdered. I'm sorry that your purity was stolen. And primarily, I'm sorry that you may be justified if you hate God. I know, may I be punished ever so severely. These things, in my frail human nature, I believe God forgives, but I find it hard to do that myself. Almost anyone would agree, should they be allowed to know, that everything you were compelled to withstand, is unforgivable.

Enough of the doom and gloom I say, let's talk about Sam. She is resettled with her job at the brokerage. Michael has another consulting job, and Tim, well, he's Tim. I'm only joking. He has settled with a full-time job, with benefits including his retirement plan. You know how he is with finance. So, March is coming around, St Patrick's day right around the corner. We used to go bar hopping, but now, I don't much like that idea. We're not going this year. We're just staying inside, perhaps we'll open a bottle of wine and call it a night.

Now that I mention it, I remember the bottle of Ca'habielli you brought us. Expensive bottle Tedward, I hope you don't do that again. That's not something most people can afford, and depending on company, can be seen as rude, so, there's your Jennifer's Life Tip for the day.

Overall, we're mostly settled in our unfamiliar environment, but one thing is still missing. We're over in DC but haven't had the opportunity to find a Church suitable for all our needs yet. We're trying. Some are too big for our liking, and others too small. We went to a small family church last week, and we didn't quite fit in. When I mean we, I really mean Tim. He's just such a Tim.

Anyway, I think now's a suitable time. Next week will have its own challenges, and I still pray for you. Every night. Dare I say, I'll write to you next week, and perhaps by then the first letter would have arrived. Anyhow, dare I say, I love you. I wish you the best, but please if you are able, tell me about you.

Are you making friends? What are their names? Have they driven you crazy like we have? I'm teary just at the thought. I really hope you're fitting in, and having a good relationship with people, despite them driving you up walls like some crazed cat. Are they treating you well? What have you been doing? Reading any Jane Austen lately? Or have you gone to bigger and better books? If there're is such a thing. . .

As always, with God's Love,

~Jennifer.

Dearest Tedward,

I trust the first letter made it into your hands, yes? I sincerely hope it made it to you, as that was for your eyes only. However, John has made it clear he will read every single letter I write to you, no matter how cumbersome it is, and no matter how verbose. He did say it was to make sure I'm not sending anything specific that could lead you to me, or I to you.

Like I'm deceptive to even think of such an idea. The nerve! All I want is to write to you in whatever Jennifer brand I think of, make you look at some clouds in the sky like Samantha's magical freight solution, falling with loads of miscellaneous freight, groceries, dry, wet, now melting ice cream, paired with some broken wine bottles and the like. Funny thing really, that joke was funnier in person, and less so as I pen it down on this piece of paper. What makes it exceptionally funny right now, though, is that when this joke was made, Sam and I were laying in the grass, over by what used to be Boston Common. Bittersweet now. But oddly enough, that's when Sam first made mention of the temperature shifting. None of us thought anything of it, and she mentioned a man, mysterious, from what I remember, maybe she remembers it better than me, but all of a sudden, when we all looked past the flowers over by the garden, there was no man, mysterious or otherwise.

Poor Sam.

She hasn't been well recently. Not sleeping all that well, and she's been a little bit of a recluse, like how I imagined you would be, alone in your apartment or house, reclusive, silent, staying away from everyone just like those cute little hedgehogs. Despite the pain their quills inflict, they're cute little critters, just like you, just like Sam. I saw her for breakfast the other day, and bags were under her eyes. You can't hide that. Even with so much makeup, short of a very experienced makeup artist, who, believe me, Sam is not.

But anyway, I could tell she wasn't herself. Michael seems okay from what I've seen of him, but even his mood isn't always as playful, I'm sure you remember. It's hard to get her to admit her problems sometimes, she can be a steel trap, as you are. But I dare say, if I can get you to open up, I can get her to come out with whatever it is that's bothering her. Tedward, I don't ask this of you lightly, but do you have any words of encouragement I could give to her? I know she hasn't said it, but I'm sure what's bothering her the most, would be those several months in the warzone.

She wasn't prepared. None of us were. Nothing could have prepared us for those things that happened. But you were there. It comes full circle now that I think about it, the world crumbling around us, and yet you were so calm and collected. We'd be dead if not for your foresight, and shall I say, the foresight God administered to you. If it wasn't for you telling Lamar to climb up and scavenge for months of supplies in the wreckage atop the sewer system, we would have starved.

I know that. Even Sam knows that. She's accepted that, but there are many things that she's still having a challenging time grasping. Those months told her a different story: that she knew all her life, a reality apart from the God she knew, and the God she loved. She still loves Him, though, but is still struggling to find the truth in all this. But I digress even just a little bit. Clearly, she isn't sleeping all that well, and she won't talk to me. Perhaps she'll open up more to Michael since they're destined to be wedded. I would like to ask, would you like to come? Be with me, and a nice little reunion, won't that be romantic?

Or if that's a bit too forward, maybe we can just settle for the old-fashioned bromance. You don't have problems with that, right, Tedward? I mean, but of course it is your decision that matters, not quite mine, but I would like equal parts of your heart paired with mine. Sorry, should I begin to sound a little sappy, but it is late when I penned this letter, and I'm really just expressing within these letters I write to you the feelings I was developing for your soul before our untimely separation. Was it for the best? I know not, but it pains me nonetheless that I couldn't say these things. I should have guessed your true feelings for me, but perhaps these are not but the ramblings of a lovesick biologist craving her wee little germs at the lab.

Well, maybe I should shut up and sign this letter before I say something I regret writing and write something you regret reading. Well, ta ta for now.

With loving kindness,
~Jennifer.

Dear Tedward,

My Tedward, you received the first letter by now, correct? It's been four weeks since the first, and I await a response, though, full heartedly, I understand it might not be possible in this life, but I will write to you, nonetheless. But regrettably, I must inform you of a few things happening. I'm unaware of any access to current events you have, or if you are in our sad state, and I implore you, should you be here, please leave at once.

Canine, or as she is now publicly known, Emily Miller, she was the one who helped escort us to safety during those hard and trying months. The one you grew to trust, and the one you elected not to kill that night, defenseless as she was. Sometimes I still wonder as to why you didn't, like everyone else? Was it because she was a woman? No. You're not like that. I know better than that. But I wonder all the same. Did you see in her eyes that she was made of something different than all the rest who recklessly abandoned you in your time of need? A woman of integrity, a trait I can vouch for; she has more integrity in one little finger than Malcolm has in his whole body.

A truly wretched man, but not one beyond saving, just as you are not beyond saving. I mean that, I truly do. I pray about it every day, and for your own sanity to come through and see the light. It is urged of us to pray for all people, for kings, and for all that are in authority; that we may lead a quiet and peaceable life in all godliness and honesty. Perhaps then, maybe God may answer our prayers. No. He will, but His answer may not be the one we want. But look at me here, again, old Jennifer going off on needless tangents again. If that doesn't tell you how befuddled my mind is right now, I don't know what will. Back to Emily, she has leaked a video displaying all the acts of cruelty bestowed upon you. How she managed it, I don't know, but I must tell you, everything you've said about your past I accept wholeheartedly as true, but to see it, is something else entirely, and I cannot fathom the pain you truly went through, the psychological torment, and dare I say, Tedward, what you experienced at the hands of us Americans, was certainly exponentially worse than the toils of war, though those weren't nothing either. For those who go into the ground without God's grace, for those who did those things to you, I'm sure there is a special place in Hell waiting for them.

But of course, only without God's grace. Like you, they can still reach it if they believe in the truth, and hopefully, not like the tragedy of he who shall not be named, perpetually trapped in bureaucracy, with nothing more than just mere death and despair waiting for them in this life, not able to take a hold of life's rewards. But you're different. You're free now. Or at least, I think. And here I am, back on that tangent. So, sadly, there was a trial. She and several other men, the Army Rangers they were, placed on trial for treason. The Rangers absolved of their crimes. Emily was not. I look at this and think of the Marathon Bomber, and how long it took for that case to get resolved until his untimely death. Decades. But with this, they moved this along rather quickly. There couldn't have been enough time for a fair trial with impartial jurors, but all that to say is Emily is being sent to be executed via firing squad.

From what I was able to gather, she was a woman of noble and upright character, a patriot with the true meaning of the word. She understood what orders were for, and the chain of command, all words of which you understand the importance of with clarity more so than anyone else. She understood that there was a time to follow orders, and a time to do what's right. She has lived, and sadly will die for these values.

But what can I learn from this? Surely, the moment you read this letter, so many things would have changed by then. Will she have been dead by the time this gets in your hands? Or will God provide some miracle by which to save her. I don't know, but what is certain is the information she provided to us kicked the hornets' nest and Black Eagle apparently is trying to shut down all the news sources. Terrible business that, and it only proves what we were fearful of. Whoever controls information, will control the populace.

History has a sad way of often repeating itself, and I fear we are down a path better left forgotten. And I wonder for how much longer Malcolm will allow us to read the Bible, without heavy revisions. Ideally without revisions at all, but perhaps that's unlikely. Or perhaps I'm just paranoid over things of which I have no control over.

Now, away from those wretched things. I'm going to start crying again with how hopeless it all seems. Samantha, I still don't have great news, but she has PTSD. We figured that to be the case, and she is seeing therapy right now. She sees him once a week after the nightmares, usually on Thursdays. They make progress, and according to Michael, she's sleeping more, but the quality of sleep certainly suffers. The bags are still under her eyes. I'm worried about her.

Tim is there to help her in the mornings until Michael and her get together for some wedding planning. They really are good to each other. Michael is going to have a rough one. He seems fine. I think, psychologically he made it out all right, but then, he has something precious to look after, much like you had something to protect during those months. And I can't thank you enough. Not for saving me, or our friends, but for that I am profoundly grateful, but rather, I can't thank you enough for making me precious to you, and Sam precious to you. Words cannot express that.

Well, I suppose some good news is in order. I managed to find another oncologist. He seemed fair and competent enough, and I started my treatments again. Hopefully, I'll finally get this leukemia rid of, with God's help of course. Mustn't forget Him. Tedward, I think it might be time to write back, but of course, I still don't expect a letter at the time of penning this down. Who knows if John even made it to the post office. Can you imagine him trying to deal with this conspiracy nonsense? I'd feel really bad for the people on the receiving end of that stick.

Well, I'm sure this letter is long enough, and much too gloomy for you. I half expect to tear it to pieces before drafting a new one entirely, but I wouldn't want to waste the paper.

With Gentleness,

~Jennifer

Dear Tedward,

Well, since you're unlikely to have read the other letter by now, it might be redundant, but worth mentioning I did mail that doom and gloom letter. John said he's been sending them off the Saturday after I've delivered them to him personally. Well, as you may have read in the news, the case regarding Emily, she was found guilty, and it still bothers me they reached a verdict so quickly, but then there's so much about what's really going on in the world that I know, and I am certain I know invariably less than what I thought I knew.

Well, that was really all I had for sad news anyway, nothing worse than that, and the execution date has yet to be announced, but the evidence weighed against her was staggering, made available to the public on all the news channels. Everyone has equal access to that information, almost like all the news channels are collaborating with one another to produce one coherent story in which everyone can agree upon.

Black Eagle scares me, Tedward, as I'm sure they scare you, but for varied reasons I wager. I think there's more darkness in them than they let on. I think that's what drove Jeff to do the things he did, calling his CO and telling him about you, the real you, not the Ted Anderson façade you placed up, albeit necessary. I wonder what he was like. Perhaps you remember. I don't know anything about this Ted Anderson, and I should like to find out, if he was someone you might consider good or not.

He must be if you were masquerading around as him, for as long as you did. But I wonder exactly what transpired, though, only if you are so willing to talk about it, such a sensitive subject, I know, but I know you can't possibly have opened up to anyone just yet, though, maybe that's not true. It took us a few months, surely you found someone to open up to. And it's not just these letters that you receive from me. But I must ask, if we ever truly see one another again, face to face, will you tell me these things? Again, I don't want to be pushy, I just want to know all facets of you, of who you want to be, and of who you were truly born to be, not this killer, not this murderer, not a soldier, or an orphan, but who you are supposed to be. I want to know; I'm dying to find out. I know, it's crazy to think about, me listening to all your problems, I never got the chance to spend time developing things you liked or moving you away from things you ought to hate.

I've got a bit of bad and good news. Well, of course you were made aware since the letter spoke of it. So, the episodes were a lot worse than what Michael and I originally thought. Apparently, she left business meetings, in the middle of them one too many times. Well, you know how that is, I'm sure, you can only do so much of that before it catches up. Businesses can only tolerate so much of that, especially coordination. I have no idea how much work she had to do to retain that account, and now, she was let go. Fortunately, with the work she put in, they were nice enough to get her a severance package, but with things going the way they are, hikes in gas, fuel, prices of groceries going up, it's kind of all over the place.

I don't have too much to tell you about Michael, but he never mentioned he whose name I won't mention. Of course, I find it odd to bring this up to you now, several months after the incident, but I think he was killed. Never heard from him. I remember reading at the time, he was admitted to the hospital. Terrible shape he was in. You know, for obvious reasons, he was placed. Then I remember he was forced into a meeting, escorted by, well, you know, but when he entered the headquarters, he never left. Terrible things are happening here Tedward, and I wish you were here.

I miss you Tedward. God, I miss you. I remember the time you ate ramen for the first time in my apartment. A slight change of pace in the cold, hot chicken broth with those nice noodles, and you slurped them all over my island. I liked that island. But sadly, I couldn't save it. I remember looking at you, just looking, there to listen when you wanted to speak, but I was in awe.

Your smile, showed with your lips pulled back, and teeth shining brightly in my adorable little kitchen. That wasn't some smile you decided to show for appreciation or a smile that I would have expected to see carved into your face so delicately. It was YOUR smile. It's not just some façade, and it meant so much to me Tedward, you'll never know. How did I, Jennifer, some germ aficionado with some unhealthy obsession over Jane Austen novels, get to be the first person to see your true face, and have it before me so that I may look upon it? You made me feel special with such a subtle act, and while you didn't intend it, and didn't realize it, you made me feel special that day.

I don't have any other updates for you regarding my personal well-being. We're still looking for a Church that fits our needs. We're still hopping around for one that would be welcoming. You'd think such a community would exist here, especially in times of turmoil, but sadly, that is not what I have found. Well, maybe this week will be a little bit different than before, and we can find one that I would love to take you to. So far, the ones I've been to here aren't ones that would be welcoming, especially not of you, for the same reason, is they don't care for young adults as much as they should.

Well, I think I must be going now, other things to do, and contemplate.

Bye-bye, Tedward,

Love Jennifer.

Dearest sweet Tedward,

I'm growing concerned you're not getting my letters. Are you getting them? It's been six weeks since the first one I mailed out with John. Are you getting them? Silly thing to ask in a letter, isn't it? I have no way of knowing if you're receiving the letters or not, or if someone is doing something crafty with them in wherever you're going, or maybe John keeps forgetting to send them. I don't know. But regardless, I will still write to you these letters. Sometimes it's the only thing that keeps me sane, and sometimes the only thing I truly look forward to doing, outside read my Bible and go through my devotions to God.

Haven't been able to keep up with the Emily incident. News hasn't been forth coming lately, but it could be related to the video she leaked out. All the news was riled up, and so did many protests make their way down to Capitol Hill. That was scary since I don't live too far from there now. I know she isn't a traitor. It's such unfair evil that has plagued her life, branding her as one, but I know God is good, but sometimes I wonder what she could have done that led to such punishment, or perhaps this reminds me of a story where Jesus went down and a man was blind and asked for help, and his disciples had the audacity to ask him about his parents sin, probably thinking something to this effect: he was born blind, he was born a cripple, surely, his parents sinned, and he is paying the price for it.

Not sure why I thought to talk about this parable, but here I am, and now that I think about it, perhaps this is one that would speak to you. As you were born without a name. You were born without a family. You were born without any semblance of opportunity, and anything you thought you might have had was stripped away. You had the carpet pulled from under you, and that just isn't fair. A fog of cynicism covers your eyes and prevents you from seeing clearly, just like this blind man did.

I think to how this contributes to Emily and poor Emily, but she had a family, she had the opportunity to climb out, and when presented with the right or wrong solution, she chose the right path, I mean that. She chose to do the right thing and had the option to march down the path of evil, dark as it were, she elected the path that, regrettably, will lead to her death, and everything, just like you, swept away underneath her.

Someone of my religious disposition might be tempted to think that your parents did something so horrible, that while they aren't paying for their transgressions and iniquities and are passing that debt to you. You get to pay for the tragedy they caused, as unrelated as they seem to one another. But that is not what I believe, for what Jesus did instead was what I perceive to be the right answer to this vague reality. Your parents didn't do anything wrong, and the blood you're born with isn't inherently evil. It's not. You're not. Emily's not. God dealt those cards to you so that He, though I struggle to see it now, will turn your lives into something good. You didn't ask for this, but none of us envy being in your shoes.

Those who don't have the same story I do might think differently, seeing it with a lens of blindness. I can't see it, for I do not have God's wisdom, but He will make something of your life, regardless of if I'm in it or not. The darkness around me swirls this way and that, and I can but blindly step forward, knowing only when and where my foot will land, but soon as I pass into the veil, will I not know where or in what my step will land.

But enough about that, I was just yappering on as Jennifers do. We're pesky little creatures who like to talk and go on rambling about things that probably don't make any sense.

Nothing's changed all that much, and Samantha has become a little more reclusive, although, with her severance pay she managed to buy and find a violin teacher. Don't ask me about the violin. I don't know where she got that. Maybe she bought it, but it's pretty nice. Needed some dusting off when she got it. You know, she didn't quite strike me as the musical type, but here we are, getting violin lessons. I'm not. Not a musical bone in my body, but I can certainly appreciate it when it comes to my ears. She plays frequently, or so Michael tells me. He's supportive of the new hobby. I have to pick one up, believe it or not, but I think I've read *Sense and Sensibility* over a hundred times now. Or expand my horizons when it comes to literature. Maybe I'll start picking up some thrillers, so, if you happen to have any suggestions on books like those, I'd greatly appreciate it.

Also, I'd appreciate a letter, handwritten from you, if it isn't too much to ask.

Love Jennifer.

Dear Tedward,

I watched the sunrise today and thought of you. Can you see it? The orange hue of the red sun expounding upon the blue sky, turning it numerous shades of orange and yellow? Rippling in the water? Things move by so fast, and I often forget to take time to look at the trivial things, the little things I still have, and especially those smaller things which takes little effort to enjoy, just like this horizon I stared at.

It reminds me, oddly, of the variations of human conditions, personalities, and moral compasses we all have. Of course, we all have our short comings, and as you know, I'm ceck full of those. Is that a word? It is now. I'll make a Shakespeare out of me yet! Or was it chockful? I don't know, but what I know now is that I need a dictionary. So, anyway, it reminded me of varieties in the hues, and the faults we all have. You know what, I'll revisit this next week. So many good things happened though. Where shall I begin?

Well, first off, should I say, we, of the four of us, found a Church we can call our own down here. It's a congregational Church, much like Park Street, though certainly not as grand but allows us our little hurrah when we want to go out. Some the scripture lessons are on the more liberal side most of the time, but still manage to be theologically sound. What am I saying? I know some of this won't make much sense to you when you read it, however long it takes for this letter to get to you. But, I must say, the emphasis on community here has been astounding, and I really wish you were here to enjoy it with us.

Sam and I, well, while she's still struggling, she does ask about you from time to time, and that's always a wonderful thing. She's still making do with those violin lessons. I must say, however deplorable her situation might be, she seems thankful, and I've been asked to be her bride's maid. Michael has been making his plans for the wedding, but they've not yet set a date just yet. So exciting. I've never been a bride's maid before! I'll ask John if you can come when we have a date, that is. I really hope he'll let you come, or whoever is in charge with whatever all this is.

Sam seems to be on the mend because of her condition, and so does Tim. He seems to be doing well enough himself, he offered to take me out to the aquarium over here, but I declined. I think he likes me, but I must say, my heart truly belongs to two people, and one of them isn't Tim. One is God, and He is primarily captivated by my heart, and the other, well, I think you know, even though it has been a while.

Tim's not such a bad person, to give him credit, and one might say he and I would be a good fit, but I must still respectfully decline. As reckless as my love is for you, it is just that, reckless. Just like you were reckless, your love for me, I know you never got the chance to openly confess it, but I think with the gift I wear around my neck every day, you were so close to expressing yourself, and that's what I really wanted. I wanted you to feel like you didn't have to pretend, didn't have to put on a special show for me, least of all out in public. But this gift here, you gave it to me out of your innocence. I know you might not see it, and might not feel it inside your heart, but the gift you gave me was out of that of a love of a precious child, unsoiled.

Knowing what I know now, you're like a precious child. One with dreams, and the sky was just the first step for you. With everything you've accomplished, the average man can only dream of doing just one of those things, and yet, you were consistent with it all. You were like a child, who wanted nothing more than to experience playtime with others. And then you became a man who wanted so desperately to fit in somewhere, but held up a mask because you feared that whoever saw what was beneath would turn you in.

Someone once told me, 'The brightest smiles bring us the greatest of joys. The loudest laughter is like a grand orchestra, and the most beautiful faces are covered in makeup, because we are okay, and everything is fine. The brightest smile is like a bandage, it looks okay, but inside the wound still festers, asking to be cut off. They say laughter is the best medicine. And the mask is our way of making ourselves look more beautiful, to reduce our flaws and hide our scars. When the smiles fade away and the bandage is ripped off; when the laughter is silenced and the music stops, when the makeup is washed away, and our mask fades, we find that we were never truly okay.'

You reminded me of this. The perpetual sadness that prevented you from feeling any felicity, any hope, and love, and of course produced in you the Hedgehog dilemma. You wanted to get close to others, but out of terror and angst of hurting others, and them, you, you stayed away. You thought people were like nightshades, deadly and lethal, and that you must stay far away. But you kept near; no stranger to death, no stranger to danger, and now, you're so far away. But not by your choice, I know that.

Looking back on it now, it's almost funny. You must have thought Sam and I lunatics for pursuing you as hard as we did. And oddly enough, it might have seemed like there was no reason to. But we saw you. We noticed that you. We saw that there was something going on behind the curtain, something that needed unveiling. No one would have guessed what lay behind the mask.

Tedward. It pains me. It hurts. I am angry. Not at God, but that God allowed you to go through all that. You shouldn't have been forced to do any of those dreadful things. I shouldn't spend much time on this, I've rambled on long enough. I'll write again to you soon.

Oh, and before I forget. Whatever foul things you did in the past, regardless of the nightmares that keep you up at night, I forgive you.

With Love,

~Jennifer

Dear Tedward,

Suffice it to say, today was an enjoyable day to stay inside and read some Jane Austen, now that I feel like going through those longer lines of lots of adverbs. Seriously though, Jane Austen has such a way of words, wouldn't you agree? She's filled with such comedy, and filled with so much awe-inspiring drama, one can only hope to be an adequate mimic of such a muse. Of course, even I cannot compare, I stopped trying years ago!

But you didn't open up this letter to read about me rave about Jane Austen and the romantic comedy that is Ms. Bennet and Mr. Darcy, oh, how you held yourself reminded me of what I imagined Mr. Darcy would be like, standing upright, smooth with the talk, and of course, filled with such verbose speeches that could only come from a Jane Austen novel, but then, that's how you chose to present yourself to us, to me. Did you get the feeling I loved my Jane Austen and read her works so fluidly as to mimic what I thought I wanted? Now, if that's what you did, I must say you did that well, and of course, going through such lengths as that, you truly are a romantic. Or pretended to be one.

I wonder, should we ever meet in person would you continue the long speeches of the façade you spent so much time building up? You don't have to do that, you know. You do, know that don't you? I love Jane Austen and all the quirks, and I love the subtle little romances inside, the character interaction and engagements with such grand parties, oh, I wish I could go to a ball. I'm sure we still have those, do we not? Somewhere. But I want you to know that regardless of how much I enjoyed that of our numerous outings together before you were taken away, should we meet again, I want you to be who you are. Not some mask, not some outing. If you're sad, be sad, I want to see the face express those emotions honestly. Will you be honest with me in such a way, Tedward?

It's been such a long time. Have you changed your name by chance? I must say, a man like you can be hard to read, but a man like you has many things about him he wishes to keep secret, but Tedward, should you not have changed your name, will you be the Tedward that you are? And listen to me plainly, I must express this, and how important it is, your secrets cannot remain secrets forever, lest they destroy you, and who are, and who you are meant to be. You know that you are of unknown origin, and these people who stole you away from me might not even know the truth. You know what it's like to have everything ripped away from you. You know the pain and turmoil those in your shoes suffer. Be a light to them. Will you? You know pain and suffering, and you can relate to them like no one else can, because you were so isolated.

Are you isolated now? Are you free? Do they allow you freedoms that my countrymen took away from you? Please tell me it is so. Please tell me you are free like a bird released from a cage, flapping your wings, spreading them, soaring ever high! Soar for me, Tedward. Whatever you want. Climb to the Heavens! Swim as deep as the deepest depths, and find the greatest reward there is! If anyone can do all those things, it's you. I believe you can do it, for God gave you the body you have, and it is impressive, and there was no mistake. Not one.

Even as I consider myself, I cannot do those things. I feel weak, Tedward. My body, there was no mistake. I still wake up sometimes with shortness of breath, and tremors. Sometimes I wake up ice cold, and others, I struggle to move my limbs, but the Lord granted me strength to make it seem like I'm okay. Heaven knows how soon it might be for me to require a walker.

I'm talking with Sam and Michael about my condition. Tim has been focusing on his career, so I have yet to reach out to him, but Sam and Michael opened their home to me, should I require it. I may take that and move in with them shortly with all the help I can muster. It's clear to me, pristinely clean, yet savagely filthy. Your body is strong, unlike mine. Your spirit is weak, unlike mine. Perhaps if my spirit could impart to you, or your body to me, perhaps we could still live as one, be of one mind and one body. That would be something. Wouldn't it? Far be it from me to suggest such a thing. Anyway, I'm still in treatment, but the Doctors who are overseeing my condition have mentioned that, though I'm lucky to be alive with the battle in Boston and whatnot, but due to the lack of care I received as a result, the disease crept in places it ought not to.

Perhaps I'm being too gloomy, and hopefully by the time you receive this letter I will be better. I do earnestly pray for you, and I want to see you. I'll see if John has anything else to say about why we can't see one another. He still won't budge on that. The nerve!

Until next time,

~Jennifer

Dear Tedward,

The Postal service isn't what it used to be. I think this is the eighth letter I've sent to you. Or ninth, somewhere in there, and I've yet to hear back from you. Surely, you must've gotten my first letter? I would have sent that to you at least two months ago. I've yet to hear back. I miss the sound of your voice, and you retreating your hand back into your pocket. It was an identifying feature of you, almost like that dreadful man at the congregation we meet. Just like he's always there, rambunctious as he is, you can feel a vacuum when he's not there. Almost like you, where it is never seen as a problem, but you're always the man with his hands inside his pockets.

Of course, I know why those hands are in the pockets. You have tremors, though forever undiagnosed, I don't know if you have something you might want to get looked at, or perhaps you're trying to hide something. Of course, anything you intend to hide must be revealed, and you can't hide those from me forever. This reminds me of when you and I played games over at my apartment, and the many times on Tuesdays at Teri Nation, good times, good times, and with many fond memories. It's where we met you. But I digress, forgive me Tedward, but I must share that I was not in the best of moods after. Sam knew something was wrong with me on that particular day, and this was well before my diagnosis. She came to me, asked me how you and I were talking, and if you were ever to come back and hang out with us.

The mask, the makeup, the laughter, the pockets. They were all fake. Just like those emotions you bottled up, and still do. I don't know what God's plan is for you, but perhaps with your new life over the sea, or wherever you are, you are allowed to talk about it more openly without fear of scorn or that Uncle Sam might come after you. Knowing everything I know now, that is the reason you were forced to keep silent, because what little freedom you had would be taken away from you.

Freedom is such a funny concept really. People die for it. People kill for it. None know that better than the armed forces, but perhaps after everything we've scene, that's an oxymoron. Doesn't hold any weight for us in America anyway. I remember reading a book once, Johanne Wolfgang Von Goethe's Elective Affinities. Such an excellent book, looking at our choices and of course, understanding what Freedom truly was, considering the human condition, perhaps you could relate. Anyway, in it, he says, "None are more hopelessly enslaved than those who falsely believe that they are free." Freedom, we take as the ability to do and think whatever it is that we want, and yet, here in America, Freedom runs in our blood. Or does it? Upon reflection, he might be calling those people who believe them to be free, are enslaved by the mere concept of liberty. When you reword the statement in something a little more straight forward, it reads something like this: Only fools believe they are free, and fools alone.

Well, if we know anything about people, we're all fools. Myself included within that mess of debauchery. Of course, don't misinterpret my words Tedward, I am still very much committed to you, regardless of if we can ever see one another again. I have never given myself to another man, nor do I intend to. Back to what I was saying, and this regrettably leads into a tragedy. Considering something we might enjoy, considering what we love, and who we love, and if we're passionately drunk on something, we may choose to pursue that individual thing, whatever it is. Blindly, we find ourselves shackled, and while the master of whatever ideals we have may be benevolent, we must remember that we ultimately don't decide what we do next for the decision has already been made.

I recall now, whatever happened to Mrs. Emily Miller. I'm not even sure if you're getting these letters, but let's assume you're not, and you somehow receive this letter before all the other ones. Let me reframe what has since happened. She was a woman of courage, and a woman of integrity, let no one have any doubts about that, even should these words be the only ones praising her name. She is also a woman of honor, and unshakable, regardless of whatever else she went through besides touring us all over Central Mass. Her character was tested numerous times, and still is. She was provided with the opportunity to kill someone important, the head officer, Barnes, of whom is no longer with us. She declined, and somehow, sent a message to all forces around and prevented something that might have resulted in both your death, and ours.

Fast forward, she was questioned and accused of treason. From what I understand, and much speculation and rumors which prevented such a case to be seen impartially impossible, assuming that's how military court works. I don't know. I wasn't in the military. Evidence was stacked against her, and rumor has it she was offered an out by Black Eagle Company. Dreadful creatures. She chose not to take it. She could have had her name cleared, but since she was a slave to her integrity, to her honor, she refused. I don't care what they say, some might say everyone has their price, and I say hogwash. Henceforth spitting on them. People who are truly beholden to their masters have no price. I suppose one might say the same of me, and God, and my devotion to you. Silly me. Why would any other girl have stayed after all this time, and without a promise to ever see you again? One might call me lovesick. One might call me stupid. And to them, so what if I am, at least I'm consistent.

Well, I can already tell I'm over halfway on the second page of this letter, and it wasn't as draining as I thought it might. Eat your vegetables and make sure you go apple picking again, make sure to wash them before consuming.

They may be covered in pesticides, insecticides, and all other form of '-cides' you're best not eating.
    Goodbye Tedward. Until next time.

    ~Jennifer

Dear Tedward,

Oh sweet, sweet Tedward. How's the weather over there? I looked up at the sky this morning, and was met with a nice cool spring breeze, the flowers are in full bloom, the dandelions sprouting with their foolishness and other such nonsense, that is bringing nutrients to other plants with shorter roots sharing the same soil. Almost like I'm a dandelion, and you're a plant with much shorter roots. How is it there?

Would you say it's dry and arid, Tedward? Or cold and clammy? Is it snowing, or do you and I have the same weather, cool with a refreshing breeze, and a light rain, and hovering over my wonderfully talented head, some light gray clouds. The water struck the ground before me, and I went for my walk. I can still walk, if you can believe it. It's just a very exhaustive exercise it is, just walking. One foot in front of the other, Tedward. Just keep moving.

I went in the grass, you understand, in, if you dare believe me, without my socks! Or my shoes and sandals. I felt the green blades of grass prickling my skin with each step, and it reminded me of how often we get caught up in our day to day lives, moving on, moving forward without engaging with the present. I remember when those cameras on our Dumb phones became all the rave, and everyone was taking pictures of their food, letting it cool down, not ideal for eating, mind you, the subtle nerve, but it reminded me of something.

Almost like an in-between. On one hand, we want to just get right down into the meal, talk about our day, talk about the past, and then the future. Ignoring the present, ignoring the present right before us. It's right there to take us seriously, and we treat it so often like a joke. It is pointless until it becomes the past. Such a trivial thing

Tedward, wouldn't you agree? It's almost like to us, the present is irrelevant until it becomes history. And that is no way to live. There is no way to learn. You of all people should understand that.

And flipping the coin to the other side, these people are so lost in the present, they desire to preserve it. Take a minute. Force everyone else at the table or wherever they're eating, to stop, listen, take a picture, and pretend it will last forever, even though it will doubtless get lost in thousands of pictures never to be seen again and completely forgotten. What we say then, we lost the memory of what was trying to preserve it, and the memory doesn't stick with us. We don't remember what it tasted like, and we don't recall the artistic expression the cook used. And the other person, just willing letting the time go by, letting the present slip away. Perhaps we could be like the cooks, cooking. Yes, present in the moment, carefully decorating the dish thoughtfully with colorful arrangements, angling everything on the plate so delicately.

I must be hungry, here I am writing about food, but perhaps I should mention something for you, something that you should know. I know for certain you may still be stuck in the past, constantly worried about what ifs, and how you could have made things better for yourself and for others, but trust me, this is perhaps something best to move on from, and I must confess I'm much better at giving advice than following it.

I'm beginning to ask myself why I'm writing this letter. It wasn't to tell you about the weather, I promise. Perhaps it was to tell you about a dream I had the other day, but now that I think upon it, you might not want to read about it just now. So much happened within those dreams, so many visions, and Tedward, I must say, I saw a beautiful flower, but I must capture it exactly right with words, real, and perhaps reawaken the Shakespeare within me and make up a whole dictionary of new made-up words. I'll call it, the dictionary of Jennifer! I'll get it trademarked!

This might be a shorter letter, Tedward, but please don't hold it against me. How can you? You're so far away! Anyway, I still love you, and I still pray for you every night when I look up at the moon light, or at the clouds concealing it.

With Adoration

~Jennifer

Dear Tedward,

I remember writing to you last week about a dream I had, and I had to put it into words. I don't understand it. Maybe you will make some sense of it, and this one is twofold, and I don't know why this dream came to me. I was under the impression that one couldn't see faces with such detail unless they've seen that person before, and a person I saw, a face, fair, flawless in such a way with gleaming eyes and a smile of one filled with such beauty, no words can possibly describe her. It was like looking at an angel cast down from Heaven with a divine purpose.

But first, I must tell you about the start of such a manifestation. Must I tell you, it started in a dark room, everything was black, and it was cold. Ice cold, colder than even the Boston winter could manifest itself, it was also painful, and we all know you can't feel pain when you're dreaming less you wake up, unless that was an old wife's tale, of which I will ignore. This dream, it was something new, something specific that I know this cannot be a normal dream, and it must mean something.

I recall the cool temperature, bringing about in the dark around me, swirling like a gracefully disrespectful hurricane. It brushed past me like ethereal hands, soft, and careful they were, forming something in front of me. The darkness. They are like clouds, no, they were clouds, and slowly, cracked the sky as sun came down, shining, illumining the darkness that was before me, filling the air with warmth, and I was comfortable again, and the pain subsided.

It is really difficult for me to express how I felt in that moment, but on my feet was grass, dampened grass with wildflowers of many kinds sprouting out on both sides of my feet, like a path. So, what was I to do but walk forward, not of my own personal agency, but because the dream dictated that I walked forward. Behind me was just darkness. Slowly, I walked, pacing myself through the soft ground, damped, and my body collapsed. I crawled, forward, you understand, for there was nowhere else to go. I was such a clutz!

And I crawled, and I crawled, and I crawled some more, and you might say, what was the purpose of it? I don't know. I was just dreaming a dream, tis but a dream, dear Tedward, but was there more to it? I assumed so, and there I was falling into a pond, wet, water filling me up as I nearly drowned, pulling myself up on a lily pad just bigger than me, big and strong enough to hold me in my saddened state.

And then it rose, avoiding all matters of logic, and clearly defying the laws of gravity as I felt light, and then in front me sprouted a large blue stem. It was like a REDWOOD! A redwood tree! It was massive! And to see it in the form of a stem, I couldn't wait to see the top, I was so jittery.

I wanted to see it. I reached the top, pulled myself on a leaf and danced through the plant life, careful not to overstep my boundaries. A warm breeze filled the air, and the scents of the budding flowers overwhelmed my senses. I can't recall ever being this enthralled by God's good creation. I wish you could have seen this! You might enjoy it; it is so peaceful here. Well, it was until I woke up.

But here lies the important piece, the one piece of which stands out above all other things, and one of the reasons I believe it to not be a mere dream, but perhaps giving me information of which I should then pass on to you, or someone else. Maybe I should see a therapist too. For I do feel grief, and I'll not hide it.

I came across another field, and in it, was a flower bud. But not a small one. This one was shaped like an egg, and it had magenta pedals, and towards the end of those petals, blue tips, much like those veins of yours. I approached it, and I touched it. The pedal was smooth, and soft. I should mention this now, but the bud was large, like a car! And then, the ground beneath me shook, and it lit up, blue again like the tips of the pedals, and beneath me, cracks in the earth. I stumbled backwards as the cracks turned into these veins, and approached the pedals of this beautiful bud, and slowly formed into it.

The bud started to bloom, and the other side of the pedals were magnificently orange like a flame. Pedals opened up, one by one, beautifully stretching out, and softly touching the ground, and the rumbling ceased. But the veins on the pedals glowed, and flashed towards me, and it was almost like looking at the sea animals underneath in the aquarium. It was THAT kind of blue. Once all the pedals had flourished, had stretched out to their fullest, there was something in the center. I think the locals call it a carpel? Not entirely sure, I'll have to get back to you on that.

And a voice cried out to me. "Come to me, Jennifer," it said. The voice was soft, warm, calm, and it belonged to a woman. So, I did what any reasonable person would do and listen to the voice that came undoubtedly from the middle of the flower and walked on the pedals. It was slippery. Highly do not recommend stepping on large pedals. When I came to the stigma, and out of it came a hand, soft and firm, it was attached to a forearm that seemed to phase through the stigma, and it touched me.

"Here I am," I said to it, and I touched the arm. The arm didn't retract, it pulled me into the Stigma. I stepped away. Probably the only thing that made any logical sense in this lucid dream, and I slipped, falling to the ground, and I watched the pistil peel open from the stigma, and there was a woman there. She was a nudist. No clothes. Beautiful, but how terribly immodest. She had silver hair, a youthful face, and a warm smile, and just like her hair, eyes also, grey.

And then I woke up without an explanation. So, I wanted to tell you. It had veins in it, so out of all the people I can talk to, you would be able to make sense of it where the rest of us can't. I think I've gone on long enough on this dream. I'll write to you next week.

~Love Jennifer

Dear Tedward,

I know I assume by now you probably haven't gotten the letter yet about the flower. But trust me when I say, the spring rain glistens crystalline through the light, and we can see beauty in our circumstances. I know the correlations of what I saw with the dream of that flower, of that woman of whom I still see with complete detail even now, a face I've not seen before. Surely that must be something important. Unless I've gone completely insane. Oh, that would be something now wouldn't it.

Tedward, how does that make you feel, after months of being apart, this being at least the third month since I've started writing these letters to you with no response, I can't help but feel neglected, but even as I penned that thought I realized something, you don't owe me anything. And inside my heart I want you here by my side as I'm sure you might still feel something for me, should you know that people still send letters in this world, this age of technology and instant gratification.

But for you.

I can wait.

I will wait.

Until such time as it is made abundantly clear that we can never truly be together, even if my brain has accepted that irrefutable fact, but my heart still clings to you. I can still see something, feel something, hope shining in the darkness, an unbreakable spear cracking what was once an impenetrable shield. But the shield I fear has since shattered. Splintered even, littered all over the once clean floor, bloodless, as chance would have it, and bloodless as I should hope it shall remain.

I must say, Sam's wedding is coming up shortly now, and after delay and delay, I must regrettably show up without my Plus One. You remember the old joke? Silly of me to even question it. Of course, you haven't. Not likely anyway. Plus Ones are people who can't get anywhere alone, and perhaps alone she should never be. Like you never should have been left alone.

Tedward, I can't imagine where you are. Or if you're even alive. John will not tell me. He won't even tell me if the letters were confirmed received or not. I suspect when I hand him this letter, something else will cross his mind as a reason not to confirm or deny anything. For God's sake, it's almost like I'm trying to find information of some private thing with the government with the way he talks, carrying himself in secret.

You don't write back. Did something happen Ted, that I should be aware of? Months come and go, and my mind wanders, wondering if you're okay, alive, dead. Are you imprisoned for something I don't know of? Are they kind to you? Did you find someone to replace me?

That last one I fear most of all because then I'll not have a place for you here, nor you for me there. Of course, that is not to say I'd much rather you in a more dangerous position, chained, dead or otherwise besides with someone who isn't me. I don't mean that at all. But I know I can't ask it of you to stay where you are if our adoration for one another must remain private, star crossed like a tragedy. I wonder, and fear, you don't think we'll end up like Romeo and Juliet will you? Both die together in a string of tragedies that which could have been easily avoided?

I really shouldn't think of such things, Tedward. I'm sorry to even mention it, but perhaps I should so that in the— what I imagine—unlikely event should you read this letter, that you will know how I feel, and what I've been going through. My speaking seems so one sided, and you seem to be only listening and not responding to the letters I write to you.

Ted. Write something. Please. I'm running out of things to pen. I'm not even sure if—no. I'll save that for another time.

Love Jennifer.

Dear Tedward,

Feel free to disregard that last letter I sent out. I'm sorry. I shouldn't have sent it. It was filled with so much more negativity that is not me, but of the Devil. I should have been praying more earnestly lately. I need to get better at that for my own spiritual well-being as I have not been feeling well as of late. Not in the last few weeks. And trust me when I tell you this, Tedward, it is not because of the lack of response from you. It is rather a result of my slowly deteriorating health. Treatments are continuing, yes. Unfortunately,, I fear that is not enough. I can feel it in my bones, my flesh slowly weakening, getting harder and harder to walk longer distances.

Something I do want to bring your attention to. Perhaps you can relate to this better than I can, and it's about the letter I mailed last week. Not the letter itself, but on how John received the letter from me. I handed it to him, and he crinkled his nose. Something I usually overlook; his eyes appeared to glaze over as if he started to cry but held it in with that toxic masculinity he tends to portray himself with. Then I asked myself, how many times did I not notice. So many opportunities wasted. I NEED to be better than this. I know I'm in pain, but that's no excuse not to reach out. When I go back to mail this letter with him, I will make special care to pay attention to the physical features, to see what else has changed. He seems a cold and calculating man, but there is more to him than what most see. He knows it. We know it. The people who support him know nothing about the man John Spadero is.

Would you behave differently than you think you would, brushing it off as if it didn't matter, just another man, another tool, such as was described of you, and much of which you claim to be yourself. But I see a person there. I see a person of whom has so much regret, so much pain, and filled with tragedy. The world itself might have been better if violence wasn't necessary. But the subtle truth is, and you know this, is it is inevitable because of the frailty of man. We created this world, and we're forced to deal with our consequences. In other words, we reap what we sow.

A movie I watched posed the question that people of good will should target people of power who do terrible things. They should fight against the Putins, the Hitlers, the Stalins of their time, and we can make the world a better place. While there may be truth to that, there will always be the underliers who will carry out their will. So, I do not think that is an appropriate solution. We cannot solve violence with violence, or else we breed a future built in blood, built in marrow, built with iron. God didn't intend it this way, but in a world filled with so much despair, so much hatred, bred by violence, there is one thing we can do.

What if the Hitlers, Stalins, and Putins never existed? Perhaps the smaller things in life, perspective, love, compassion, and a Godly stance on what it is they should render would allow those people some warmth in their hearts. Perhaps if people actually loved their neighbor as they ought to, they wouldn't fall through the cracks of obscurity, and in a desire of attention, grow out their hatred to those around them, and perform the most heinous acts imaginable. I remember a quote from General Omar N. Bradley, "Wars can be prevented as easily as they are provoked, and we who fail to prevent them must share the guilt for the dead." A hammer if you will. Those in power to prevent these things ought to take the opportunity.

So, I ask you, what would you do in my position? Call him later in the evening when undoubtedly, he's busy, force him to talk about what he's going through, and what he's feeling maybe? Does he feel isolated? Does he have people to talk to in his time of need with his shady organization, of which, perhaps he's just a mere pawn? But he spoke with some authority given the agreement which you and I, and Sam, Michael, and Tim were all forced to agree to without any agency or freewill given the circumstances.

I'm going to see the oncologist on Monday. I thought you should know that. We're doing some more testing to see what else I can do for my treatment as I am still waiting for an appropriate donor. My condition is worsening, and I implore you. I know you may not believe, but that's okay, but if you wouldn't mind also being a prayer warrior for me? Pray for healing for my body, and for this sickness to go away. Perhaps one more time, one more prayer each day can make me feel better. God is listening to me, as surely, He does to you, even if you don't believe in Him. Please consider this, for me, Tedward? I would appreciate it.

Regardless of what you should do in this situation, should you be presented with one such as this, I implore you, Tedward, that you reach out to him or her, and be a friend. Listen. You don't have to say much, all you have to do really, is listen, and respond to anything that requires an emotional or a physical response from you. I would also implore you to open the Bible every now and again and read that tome, though considered dull by most, I think you'll find something there worth holding on to.

It's a special book. One that people have spent the last two thousand years dissecting meaning of. And of course, led countless astray for people who read the Bible quite literally, and most of which is historically accurate, and those parts should be read literally, but there are others that false witnesses read, pull out of context, and take it for face value, perverting the will of God. And you just can't have that. And such behavior is deplorable, and pulls people further into Hell than out, further into the dark, and away from the light.

The darkness becomes almost too comfortable for them than the truth is. Tell them they read something incorrectly, and they will slam it into your face. Present them to the truth kindly, and only then can a kindling flame of truth be produced in such a way that edifies others, and is pleasing to those involved, and to God, regardless of any curses one might be forced to live with and reconcile. You've known darkness for too long, Tedward. You know that. You understand that better than most. I know that. Please, don't dawdle in the dark, for in the darkness, you'll never truly find your way.

Well, this letter is getting quite long. I'll write to you next week.

Ta ta for now.

~Jennifer.

Dear Tedward,

Forgive me for being solemn in this letter today.

I mailed the previous letter, and I paid attention, much closer than I usually do. John's eyes watered, and his nose crinkled. He told me he mailed the letters but received no confirmation the letters had yet been received, but he seemed sad. Despairing even. I asked him what was wrong, and he turned his expression to a smile, as you do when you don't want to talk about something. I wonder if you and John might have a good relationship with so many similarities. The only difference is he seems to have a level of politeness that you lacked when sincere.

But please don't take that the wrong way. I know what I said can be harsh, but the truth is, nonetheless. The truth. Something you might also have a skewered understanding of. I know in this world, the truth seems subjective, leading us down several paths of ambiguity, and within that, furthered the hatred we find ourselves, and of course, our neighbors, our friends, causing division and strife with one another when there need not be. The truth is the truth, and it is objective. One might say that the sky is blue, but the truth is, for those who see colors normally, the color of the sky appears blue in our sight, and generally accepted that the sky is blue. There are others who will die on the hill. And that just isn't true at all.

While it may be true that our perception of the sky is blue. We mustn't forget that the sky is essentially nothingness. We physically can't see empty space, and our mind processes the light from the sun to fill in the space. Just think about the space in front of you. There's air there. You can't see the individualized molecules or how they're being bonded together into something that you and I can breathe into our body. We can see the color of physical things, unless it's transparent like water or the air that we breathe, however, when we stare up into the sky at night, gazing at the stars, it appears black through the absence of direct light, and lit up by the moon reflecting the sun's light on the other side of the earth. And our perceptions change as to what we think the color of the sky should be, much darker than the hue of light during the day with the bright yellow sun.

The sky is filled with so much empty space, but our perception of it changes based on the other hues of color in the air, and the perception of which we choose to filter out those hues. Darkness is black, and the light of the day is blue, but the fact remains, it's empty space. Now, that doesn't make it any less pleasing to look at, now does it?

Ted, I know about the life you've lived. I lived it with you when you were by my side, and I know that the people around you spoke nothing but lies and lies and deceit was all you knew. Trust me, when Sam and I spoke with you, it was nothing but the truth, and our perception of you leading to some semblance of truth, regardless of the façade of that smile of yours, that everything was fine. The world isn't fine, Tedward, neither are you, and neither am I.

There.

I said it.

I'm not fine, Tedward.

It's been almost six months since we've been uprooted from Boston. Six months, and the damage is finally being recovered. The coastline is beginning to look like nothing happened to it. But what of Tim, Me, Michael, and Sam? As I mentioned, Sam is doing better, much better, I saw her smile the other week, for what seemed to be the first genuine smile in months since those horrible things happened. Michael seems to be okay for the most part, but when I saw him, I knew something was itching at him. Tim, likewise, seems fine as he's working on his career here. Lovely person. And me, what about me? I miss you. I have Samantha, but I miss you. I miss seeing you, hearing your laugh, some genuine, some forced, but I missed that about you, as relatively predictable you were, I couldn't always tell if the smile you were about to curl up about your lips was going to be genuine until the lips themselves curled, and I could see the true feelings pouring out of you.

But that's not all Tedward. It was a matter of three months, I think, since Russia bombed the coast. It's been two months after since I've thought to write these letters to you. And another three or four months afterwards. Those three months without the treatment I needed took a toll. And getting resettled in was simply fine, but it took time to get the proper treatment, and still, without the appropriate stem cells, of which are still on such short supply, I don't think my body appreciated me being careless.

I can feel it, Tedward. My body. It's breaking. The blood vessels are swelling up, and I'm prone to infections which may result in further disease, treatable or not. I fear even a cold could ruin me. I feel my bones weakening. I'm not going out on runs anymore, but even on my walks, I feel like I've just run a marathon. I'm getting weaker. Tedward, I pray to God that He will take this pain away from me, but it only gets worse. I feel like my prayers aren't reaching Him, or that He's ignoring me. Am I to be like Job? You don't know who that is, so me comparing myself to him wouldn't mean anything to you, but I'm terrified. Ted, I know you're strong, can you lend me some of your strength please? I desperately need it. More than anything else, I think.

Bye Tedward,

~Jennifer

Dear Tedward,

Where do I begin? Well, let's start with the sad letter I sent last week, and again, John looked sad, but he didn't say why. His assistant, her face was downcast as she looked at me too, as I handed the letter to him. She looked terribly dreadful, and unfortunately, I wasn't presented with an opportunity to reach out to her either. I had to move very quickly and get out of John's office. Probably some meeting he had to address that he was late for, since, you know, he had to deal with me. Pesky Jennifer and her desire and compulsion to write letters to you. Well, no matter, I'm sure John will open up eventually.

So, Sam's wedding is coming up. Just two more weeks actually. It's so exciting. I may have forgotten to mention to you that Sam, as you might have guessed, requested me to be her maid of honor. Tim of course selected to be the best man but try not to be too hard on the man. The tremendous shock of being stuck here in DC got him most of all. We can make calls to our family, that much was good, but only with the government issued phones John provided to us specifically. Anyway, it will be a joyous occasion!

I should also mention, last week was an awfully bad week for me. I'm doing much better now. Not so much bleeding, but the fatigue wore off. I managed to run around the block if you can believe it. Still hurt though. I must suggest, one ought not run into a full sprint just because you can. Terrible business. I am feeling much better and it was incorrect of me to despair to you last week. I was being tested, you understand, by God Himself.

You know, there's an old saying, and I cannot recall from whence I came across it. It went something along the lines of, "The teacher is always silent before the test." That was me last week. I was a student, struggling to take an exam, and that exam obviously being life, and I was in pain, I was stressed, and filled with so much anxiety it might rip apart the walls of

Troy. And I despaired. Truly, I did. I can't say I fell as deep as you did, but who could know the depths of the darkness of your own soul? I try to, and I think I understood better than anyone else, but even I cannot fully grasp it.

And this reminds me of the darkness you've expressed and showed to us during those painful nights. You showed us the real you. Brooding, sarcastic, short, disrespectful, vulgar. You are a man who knows blood on his hands and seen life leave their eyes. You've created widows, orphans, childless parents, and cut dreams short. But through it all, you have one thing, and even if that's only towards me, and Sam to a degree, you have love. Hold on to that, I implore you, hold on to that. When you don't have hope, when you don't have anything good going for you, which seems to be the theme of your life, hold on to Love. If you accomplish remarkable things, but have not love, it is all worthless. Saint Paul would tell you that. Love abounds in you; you just need to nurture it. Sure, the seed might be shriveled up, but it isn't beyond saving.

Just a faint little mustard seed. Small, pointless to many perhaps, but when it grows, it grows like a mountain. Very influential. Much like you. You might be just one person in the cog of a machine of which we all reside, but we fail to see how big this machine is. You are but one, and while I might be a bigger seed perhaps, you have a smaller one, but my bigger seed will only grow so far, and my fruit may be all but diminishing. Yours, however, will make this machine run, and go the course down the course it sails. I'd like to see what you do with this machine, Tedward. I'm certain you'll do such wonderful things with the gift of influence that you have.

But I suppose first you must make a step in the right direction. I know you have love untapped and unnurtured, and I suggest you water it. For I know that there is a tree, already planted and grown of hatred inside your chest. It pumps, rapidly at all times with the unjust deeds performed on your body, performed on your heart, performed on your soul. Any person in your shoes would have broken under such nefarious conditions. But you survived. No living person should have had to survive those conditions. And it angers me that it happened. But we must move forward. Let the hateful tree whither and nurture this tree of love. You'll find it so much better in the end.

Speaking of, back to the wedding. I just got measured for the dress, and I can't wait to show it to you. I know, I'll get my picture taken in the dress, and send it with the next letter, and of course, have it signed as only I would do, send something so vain in a most careless way. Don't fret. I'll make sure you get it. She has her white dress, and I'm not sure how Michael's going, probably the same tux as every other wedding, maybe he'll change it up, wear a nice vest, a cowboy hat, or even a bow tie. Kind of comically disgusting now that I have that image stuck in my head now. Anyways, here's too good health, and I'll talk to you next week.

I love you Tedward,
~Jennifer.

Good morning, Tedward!

Since I've no way of knowing if you're even receiving these letters, I simply wish I could just wisp you from wherever you are to me. Oh, Tedward, wouldn't that be romantic? To repair a fractured faerie tale? Of course, this would be an odd fairy tale where the damsel is rescuing the prince.

I'd read the heck out of that fairy tale. I should write it, but I am no Jane Austen, as much as I sometimes pretend to be. But maybe, we already lived it, you know, in a weird dysfunctional way, part of our little family. I still talk about you, to Sam and Michael, occasionally Tim. Oh Tim. He's such a Tim, you know. Always spitting water on people's carpets. And messing with beans. Now, don't ever trust him with beans. He spills them all over the place.

Now, oh what can I talk to you about this week? Since these letters have undoubtedly been one sided, there is only so much more I can write. Without a response as we lose things to talk about. But I can speak of the wedding. Oh, Tedward, you should have been there. She looked beautiful, and we had a nice outdoor bonfire, of which, John supervised. You'd never know it, but he was there, hiding in the crowd, eyes fixated on me, Tim, and Michael and Sam.

Anyway, you should have seen the two. They twirled around on the floor. Well, the grass, freshly cut, mind you. The flowers were in full bloom. The skies were clear, and not so gloomy, the moon was shining brightly with all the stars. I counted the stars, and the bright ones, and I saw Leo in the sky. The big scary, brave lion. He was in the sky, roaring at my enemies. Roaring for passion, roaring for you. The love I have for you, I cannot contain it, and some might call me crazy for pining after you all this time. One might ask me, "Jennifer, it's been half a year, get over him already," but I don't want to. I know, that's selfish of me, but can I have this one thing? It's all I want. Well, that and Jesus.

If you couldn't tell by the contents of this letter, it's been a momentous week! Physically I'm doing okay. I could have danced, but I didn't want to. Not without you. Oh, Tedward. You know what I'm about to ask you. Don't you? When, or if we see one another again, will you do the honor of taking my hand and dance with me under the stars? Would you do me that favor? Well, I suppose you can answer that in person, or not at all, with the way these letters are going.

Anyway, the only Debbie Downer of this, and no offense to anyone named Debbie, Downer, or Debra, is their honeymoon. They can arrange it, but you guessed it, with it comes John Spadero. Good old congressmen, so they can take their honeymoon when and where he says. Honestly, it's almost like he doesn't trust us to not speak of you know what. Like I know of anything of the sort.

Though I would suppose in the grand scheme of the Almighty, it might not make a difference. You see, from what I've gathered, there are two worlds, one on top of the other. One is subservient to the other. My world, and my God are being served by the other, and we are being served(what, I do not know) by you and your world, whatever that is. Whenever I ask, John scolds me harshly, like a judge to an unruly defendant. It's like he doesn't want me to know about the truth, and whatever this other world exists for some purpose unknown to me, and at least until recently, unknown also to you.

Tedward, can you tell me about it? It's okay if you can't, I thought I'd ask. My scientific curiosity is getting the better of me, now, of course I can't know everything, but of course I'd like to learn about it.

The skies were clear. I told you that before, but are they clear where you are? Can you see the stars? The moon? The clouds, the sun? Do you hear animals or birds chirping out the windows, and feel the wind caressing your face? Can you feel warmth in your blood, and strength in your bones? Tedward, all these things and much, much more should you be seeing, but I can't tell if we're looking at the same things through the same lens as I imagined we once were. Do you feel loved where you are?

When we found you, you were pleasant, but isolated. You wanted that, didn't you? Isolation was comfortable for you, and you even put up a front as if to tell us that you're okay, and you didn't need any additional friends. Well, a spun tale of lies that was. You know it, I know it, Sam, Michael, Tim, and Erin—she knew it too. We all did. Of course, she knew you mainly through work until Sam and I, though unintentionally caused you to quit your job, and for that, I'm sorry. I know it was good for you to do that, but can you forgive me? Anyways, I must get going. I need to get this letter to John before he departs from his office.

Ta ta for now!

~Jennifer, with love.

Dear Tedward,

To say that my blood is boiling wouldn't do justice to the emotions raging on through my veins, and I'm holding it in as I write this, but I realize that it isn't healthy. I apologize if it seems I'm taking it out on you. My blood boils, and I can almost feel the steam pouring out of my ears, filling up this room with so much pent-up anguish, writing away. Even the pen rattles with an iron grip. I know I haven't a right to be angry at this, but I am regardless. I'm not sure if there is a just way to go about resolving this.

Well, I should start here at least. After Sam's wedding, and them awaiting approval from John to go on their honeymoon, I had a little mishap. I wasn't doing too well, you see, bones were cracking, and I took a tumble down some stairs. Sprained an ankle and a few minor cracks, but nothing too major. Patched up nice and firm, but unfortunately, I wasn't able to get to John to hand deliver this letter to him for him to mail you.

So, Sam checked in on me and brought me some white chocolate. My personal favorite, and I stuffed my face into it like a child. Oh, those were good days back then. She asked me if there was anything she could do for me, and I handed the letter to her and told her to give it to John so he could mail it to you. She obliged quite affectionately before leaving me with a warm hug to end the day. I've moved in with Sam and Michael, by the way. They'll be keeping an eye on me until such time I am removed from this thorn at my side.

So, she went to John instead. John likely assumed she was there to bully him into approving their honeymoon request, but no. She was on a mission. She approached the office, so she told me. She handed the letter to him, and she told me that John took the letter, and placed it on his desk. Apparently, Sam wanted to kill two birds with one stone and proceeded to bully him for the honeymoon request.

Apparently, things got heated in the office, and not in an effective way, you understand.

So, in the office, tucked away was a box. She found it tucked away inconspicuously. I was too naïve, and too worried with my condition to take note of such things. She went over and kicked it. The box toppled over and with it, so did the contents inside. Sixteen letters. My letters. The man, I want to call him names, but I mustn't. I want to. I want to dislike him, I want to hate him, but he never sent you any of those letters. They remained unopened and untampered with. But why he said he was going to send them, and he didn't. It just infuriates me to no end.

John didn't let Sam leave with the letters and was promptly escorted out. The nerve. He never let us have those letters back. He never mailed him. Oh, Tedward, it pains me that even now, as I write this for my own therapeutic tendencies now, I know you'll never see this letter, and my blood boils and ears steam with the result of that sudden realization, and you and I are oh so far away, and further now since the gap to communicate has now been severed. Who am I kidding? It was never there. I was a fool.

My heart is broken. My body is breaking. My spirit is yet to be broken, but that time I fear is drawing near. I must confess, that I do want you by my side, allow us to sit on the grass in this heat, the warm weather with warm summer rains carelessly berating us as we stare up at the Heavens, and I realize something, that you and I were, though expressed it in oddly unique ways, star-crossed lovers that could never be. You are my Romeo, and I your adoring Juliet. Fortunately, we don't have the politics of family feuds looming over our heads to push us into tragedy, when back then when the agreement was thus settled, I became dead to you already.

Not out of some fear of me abandoning you, you know I cast my spirit to you wherever you go. But you can never truly verify the truth. You do not know if I am alive or dead, much like Schrodinger's cat. Whether living or dead, is irrelevant until you open the box. But how does one open a box of which he has no knowledge of, or how to get said box? My existence is a tried enigma, of which there is no easy solution.

And as of the moment Sam told me about the altercation between them, you thus became dead to me. Not merely because you are factually dead, I know not, but like I am to you, you are to me. Schrodinger's cat. I too cannot verify if you are living or dead. But perhaps I can. Why else wouldn't John have discarded those letters? Why isn't he sending those letters? I'll confront him about it this week when I go. I'm well enough to, I think. Maybe I should just keep sending Sam until I can walk more confidently instead.

Part of me still wants to hate him for this, hate him for the things we're forced to endure, time away from family up north and so on. He has intentionally kept you away from me, and me away from you, and it seems with each passing week, the distance between us grows, and is not pulled nearer together. Again, I don't know of the severity of us knowing what it is John and you are all about with those creepy crawling things on both of your arms, glowing in many colors for reasons unknown to me, but must I say, that regardless of that, it doesn't affect how I feel about you, and it does affect what I know, and that is nothing. Therefore, I must forgive John, as much as I don't want to. God calls me to do it, and so will I.

Tedward, regrettably I feel like my next letter will be shorter as I don't expect to report on much except my healing with the bone fractures and the sprain. I was fatigued last week, hence the fall, and my added stress from John didn't help. I trust that whenever you see this, if that is, that you find it in yourself to forgive me for all I have done to you, and all I have not done for you that I should have, and to please forgive John Spadero for his incompetence.

I love you.

~Jennifer.

Good morning Tedward,

I'm sitting at home as I write this. The window is cracked open, and I can smell the breeze coming in. The hot tea at my side, green tea, I must say, just a dash of milk is exactly right. Yes, the perfect cup of tea, and I don't care what anyone says about it. It's right for me.

Now, I know after last week's episode, I might be deterred from writing a letter. I will get John to mail these. I will. It might be the last thing I do but do it I must. I will send Sam again this time, as I shouldn't be doing too much walking right now. From the fall last week, it got hurt pretty darn good. Bruised everywhere. Had x-rays and all that, but nothing alarming. There are no solid breaks, and those can take a long while to heal and get the reset back in place. The sprain is much better though. I can walk on that without issue and even walk short distances.

I might also mention, that last week, Sam and Michael, yet again were delayed on their honeymoon. John didn't approve anything, and apparently via letter, said that they should make a honeymoon here locally in DC. Well, that just isn't very romantic at all. Congratulations, here's some trash. This is only the finest trash heap in all the land. Well, that and New York. Dallas is a close third.

Anyway, I don't often talk about me getting a donor, but just as you would have guessed, still waiting. Help is in short supply, as well as this donor and the necessary cells I would need to fight off my leukemia for good and feel somewhat normal again. I don't think I appreciate being normal enough, having my bones work, my body working the way it's supposed to and go on longer runs that I can't go for anymore. And there are other things which I did with you, apple picking, that I couldn't enjoy as much as I would have liked. Trust me, I'd love to go picking some apples with you again, under different circumstances.

When I called Sam over the other day and told her I'd still be writing these letters to you at first, she nodded and smiled sadly, as if just to let me process my own grief in a typical Jennifer-like fashion. In her eyes I saw the look of someone who was looking at an old friend going senile. I felt it, hitting me like a hammer. Me having Leukemia doesn't help with that, but I suppose I'll talk to her about it later, just to address that. I can't continue to live here if my friends think I'm senile, and quite frankly, on the way out with one foot already in death's door. I'd much rather not have to think my friend have any undue pity on me.

Moving onward, I asked her since I still don't trust my body enough to make the track right over to John's office this week to send the letter. I'm going to have Sam do it. When I asked her specifically to give it to John, she was belligerent. She didn't like the idea and told me I was being childish. She said writing the letters was enough, but to continue stamping them, and sending them to John, who we know is not sending the letters, she said it was pointless.

Maybe it is. I don't care. I don't hate him for it. I forgave him of that folly situation and moved on, but I will keep trying to get all these letters to you. Every single one. So that you may know, before it's too late, that this cat is alive. And I'm not going anywhere until I can verify for myself that you are also alive and kicking. Well, maybe not kicking.

It's been a while since I've told you what I've been reading. I recently delved into a translation of Dante's Divine Comedy, and oh, that was a mistake. There is nothing funny about this book, and they have the nerve to call it a "comedy," Good Lord, they should have more respectable tact for such things. But the idea of a literary comedy is not one for laughs and giggles, rather, so many dreadful things can happen to us, but in the end, whether those things are tragic, lukewarm, or good, it all ends well. My life will be a comedy, for even when I die, I get to be wrapped in God's arms, warm, and get to do whatever work He has set for me in Heaven. Not sure what a researcher will do, but I'll take what I can get. As for you, I fear, hopefully wrongly so, that you will have a different path, down the line of tragedy, where the worst things do happen, and there is no recovery. It's a fear I have, so I will say this, hopefully, to avert any further tragedy.

You should forgive those who wrong you. You should have patience with the unbearable and persist in the greatest of trials. I know you know how to do that last one really well. Learn to love. Without me. I fear that we will never touch again, never again see one another face to face, and there is a strong possibility that these letters may never see your eyes. I hope that last bit isn't true at all.

Well, I must be going. I'm running late to Church already. I'm praying for you still, and I love you still.

~Love Jennifer

Dearest Tedward,

It pleases me to say that Sam delivered the mail. As far as making it to the post office, well, that is another story. And I'm sure when I speak to John since I found out about him not delivering the letters, I doubt he'll be straight forward as to the reason. Politicians never are. The world would be a much better place if we just stopped bickering, spoke what we meant without dealing with all the jargon designed to confuse all others outside that field. We'd separate fact from theory, and theory from hypothesis.

Still no donor. Same sad story but with a different tune with more optimism than I've been filled with of late, and much more can I say, I feel much better. I can walk a longer distance, and I've not been plagued with fatigue this week, wonderful business. I think I'll deliver the letter this week myself to John, and see what he says, how he says it, what information, new or old he'll give to me that I might have something more to talk about in these verbose letters.

Sam and I had a long discussion this week. Now I'm not sure if I should mention it. Such harsh words I have for my brothers and sisters within a context you might not understand. I really should stop trying to bring you into my problems, but I want to share them with you. Perhaps I should leave this for a conversation we have in person, perhaps that would be more appropriate where the words I say will have some time to cool off, and my heart will have settled. Again, this is assuming I can ever truly see you again.

You really have a way with words, don't you? Make things sound harsh, hitting people with the sense of realism that which can only truly be found in people who lived lives not censored by the world. Often, we find ourselves contemplating what to believe, and who to believe. What I have seen, with my own brothers and sisters of Christ, is that most would rather resort to hatred, rather than love. One asked me, why do people think He's a God of love? And it clearly brought me to something that said God hated those who do evil. But that was a psalm on which that was written, and thus translated, and I do not believe it to be a mistranslation. However, Psalms, like songs and poems, ought to be read with utmost care as they are rarely every written to be read literally. They pushed this down on me at church, and I pushed back at them. If God hated us, who sins, then at what point was there to anything? God hates us, and the New Testament happened which is not consistent with that belief at all. Anyway, the church squabbles. Always a pain in the neck. I think you and I both know I don't need any more there or any other part of my body.

Back to Sam, rather, and not related to any of our churchly activities, I must say, she had an episode the other day. A PTSD episode. To be frank, it was more and more consistent since Michael, and she just got married and were living together. I was away at a Bible study when it happened, and she flipped over some eggs on Saturday morning. We spoke to her quite a bit, and she went up and started playing the violin in the late-night hours of the night in the attic. She's gotten better. She truly has. No need to worry about her yet. She's strong, she likes to pretend to me, but thinks she isn't. She's much stronger than she herself gives her credit for.

Well, that's my update, and I've resolved upon myself I will deliver this letter myself to John and see what he has to say. I will forgive him to his face as they will be like coals atop his head.

I love you.

~Jennifer.

Dear Tedward,

I don't think I've asked how you are in quite some time. How are you? Are you doing well? Are you listening to nature? Fall is coming up shortly, are there auburn, golden, red leaves forming on the ground, and pavement where you are? Is it raining? Do you find comfort in these little, trivial things? Are you studying, or perhaps you retreated into the comfortable setting of an office somewhere, trading stock and options and delving into foreign markets of which I, of course, know nothing about. I never really had an interest in that sort of thing.

The field of finance has a way to make the world move. You understand that, arguably better than anyone. And nothing is moving faster than Black Eagle Company. The armed forces are still in disarray. To say they terrify me is an understatement. They've been spreading out lies about the execution of Emily Miller. There was an uprising, I think, when it happened, and Emily Miller allegedly moved south beyond the Rio Grande River outside the Black Eagle zone. They couldn't go in without provoking a war, and I think public opinion has sway over him.

BE reminds me of a few things. Primarily, fascists of Nazi Germany, and the KGB of Russia. They're spreading lies, and people are buying into them faster than hot cakes. Flyers pouring out of the sky. Honestly, you'd think there'd be more outcry for carbon emissions and needless printing of paper. I'd like to say nobody reads flyers anymore, but regrettably I saw many people reading the fallen documents like leaves, and the government isn't doing anything about it. Freedom of speech, they say, or some other bother of which they hold supreme over everything else, including whatever faith they thoughtlessly proclaim with their lips. A sad state of affairs.

There used to be a time where I was proud to call myself an American, but regrettably, it's become a cesspool that has since encroached upon my life. And those that were also corrupted, likewise would call my brothers. Far too often, in the profane they cry out to God, and He listens, but barely, I should think as they continue to spout off hatred towards one another, and towards others. They speak the truth, or so they say, but they speak it not in such a way that one would receive grace, and it became rotten hate. I remember oddly, a quote from someone who was not a believer, and I recall not who it was, but the quote was this:

Call it like it is hate the Sin and the Sinner.

A hammer to the face if ever there was one, and for once, I agree with whoever said that. I don't hate the sinner. I hate sin, and I speak the truth with my lips in such a way that one might receive the Grace of God, and be open to Him, as I was with you. I was gentle, kind, and listened to all that you had to say for the terrible things you did. But should anyone else profess their love for you in the way I have, but be distorted by no small amount of hate, you undoubtedly would have taken a different path.

I came to you with grace and compassion. These others of whom I refer, which are not just in one Church, but all of them—and some are louder than a collapsing building, or even a dropped bomb—will have no qualms calling you a devil, a murderer, and one beyond redemption. They would have no problems calling you a baby killer, and God should just abandon you. You're worthless, they believe that, of which I have no doubt. But all those things, you are not.

Don't believe a word of it! I love you. God loves you. Samantha, Michael, Tim, they love you too. You're part of our dysfunctional little family. It wouldn't be us without you, and even when you seem so far away, and fueled with uncertainty, we cannot forget that you are part of us.

Of such grace that I extended to you, I also extended it to John. Last week when I went to his office to mail in that letter. It was late at night, and he told me his assistant she was taking out the trash. His trashcan was full, so I don't know what he was talking about. Anyway, I gave him the letter to mail, and he placed it in a drawer. He asked me to leave, and I confronted him to his face, and told him that I knew he wasn't sending the letter.

He swore at me. Not something you do to a lady. He said if I knew, why'd I bother to send another letter and go through the effort of writing another one? And here I am, writing yet another letter that undoubtedly will just go in that box. Unfortunately, I couldn't yet verify the location of the other box which held the rest of the unmailed letters. Do you know what I said to him? No. Of course you don't. Because he didn't mail the letter. I told him, because I knew he didn't send the letters, and that it was incorrect of him to do that, make me believe he was sending the letters when in actuality, he was just holding onto them. I told him that while it was wrong of him to do that, make promises without keeping them, and underneath false pretenses, I forgave him for it, nonetheless.

I may have also proceeded to proclaim to him that I will continue to write letters until he finally mails them to you. I'll annoy him if that's what it takes.

Sorry for the doom and gloom.

Anyways.

I love you Tedward!

~Jennifer.

Good morning Tedward,

I can still feel the cool breeze blowing through this window, hearing the rain drops strike the side of the houses, ripples in puddles, crystalline. Ripples. It's amazing what one drop can do. Pour one drop of water into a cup, it creates ripples, endless waves that go out throughout the distance until the force loses its kinetic energy. Eventually, the range of its influence will cease as the kinetic energy runs out, and converts itself to potential energy, limited, theoretically to what it could do, and not what it's doing.

I think we tend to find kinetic force to be powerful, more so than potential, but then, something with potential could be infinitely greater than anything we can physically see moving things in front of our very eyes. We look at the pitcher. The speed at which he throws the ball can be great, it could be small, but until it's released can we calculate the amount of force it has behind it. But the ball could be thrown poorly, or it could be thrown at greatly exceeding speeds of over one hundred mph. Or it could be a curve ball, a changeup, a breaking ball and so on.

So too like the violinist at the recital. I spent some time at one with Samantha the other day. A violinist, if you don't know them or who they are, is a blank slate. You don't know what their potential is until they start pulling the bow back and forth across the strings and it sings a tune filled with a beautiful melody. We are often in awed by the kinetic because we can see and verify with our own eyes how great they are, but we're hardly exposed to how great they could be.

To say you are a small drop in a big pond is an understatement, dear Tedward. I'm sure you recognize that, but you have influence on those around you, good and bad influence, whether upon me, Sam, or now, with whomever you happen to be with, and whatever project you're doing is bound to have a big splash, in a small pound. You are much closer to a rainstorm, gloomy, sure, but filled with so much kinetic energy, it's difficult to contain it all, difficult to control sometimes. But that kinetic energy was converted from potential, and it is no mistake to suggest that you have shown us your potential, and maybe we haven't seen all of it, we have without a doubt, seen most of it.

And just like you, that violinist sang. Not literally. The music, the melody from one of Bach's pieces was beautiful. I highly recommend listening to Bach, or perhaps even some of Vivaldi. Antonio Vivaldi and his song, Winter, have plenty of excellent covers of that beautiful classic. Perhaps you can find some piece in music, or some in some other art, whether it be writing poetry or prose, composing songs, or performing some music, drawing, painting, there's all sorts of ways you can channel your thoughts in such a way to avoid outright telling anyone what you're feeling. I think the important thing is, you need to find a way to express yourself more passionately and let the feelings and thoughts process.

Tedward, I know you've experienced a lot. I know you're oppressed with guilt, regret, a tremendous amount of loss and suffering. Everyone who knows you, knows that. But as far as I know you, you don't easily open up about these things, and there might not be many other Sams or Jennifers in the world that would open you up like an egg as forcefully as we did. Though it did make for a messy meal for all parties involved. I think it might be fair to say, especially after all this time, you still haven't opened up, and you're being pent up.

That is no way to live. It is unhealthy. Like if you shake a soda bottle way too many times, it will explode and is destructive. I know you hate violence, and yet, that is all you know. Violence shouldn't be the first answer, but it is the only answer you've known to give, for that was what you were exposed to. What are we to do with something like that? Well, most people here would say you should be locked up, and never see the light of day. You're too dangerous to be left alive, just echoing their thoughts.

But that is not what I think. I don't believe anyone is beyond redemption. You are not beyond redemption, and there's a God that loves you. However, skewed you received it, I believe He loves you, nonetheless. Should you receive grace from Him, you should share it with others. I know I might be in the minority here since churches, the one I go to is no exception to that, share a legalistic view, meaning, you sin, you're worthless and ought to be cast out to dry, and shot out in the back never to be seen again. I've already seen such behavior with others trying to rationalize the government's wishes and their motives for hiding Emily's execution.

Our church is broken. The original shepherds went off on their own tangents, murdered by devilish thoughts and creatures, violently churned them out to be someone no one recognized. And others follow suit following a theology of exclusion and hatred. Judgement, and those things are to be left for the Lord, not us to follow. I must confess, my spiritual wellbeing hasn't been great lately because of it, but I still pray every day, and sometimes, not all the time, but sometimes, it reminds me of how close God is with my life. These are the things I constantly pray for:

My spiritual and physical health, treatment and doors open for the right donor. Sam's health, and her marriage with Michael. All of our work. I pray for the Church life that we may all pray fervently and seek the Lord first above all things, for forgiveness of my sins, of which, I must confess are many. I pray for you, and your spiritual, mental, and physical health. I also pray that one day we can be united once again, if only it should be platonic, and not romantic. I suppose, should that be the case, I should stop quoting Jane Austen to your face. Well, must I confess then, I do still love you, but I am beginning to see, while I should have seen it before, that God doesn't intend for you and me to have a future together. I accept that. Or pray to.

I can already tell this letter is getting much too long, so I must bid thee adieu, until next time. And yes, yes, I understand. John probably won't send this letter either, but I'll still try, and annoy him. Hopefully, I can annoy him enough where he will finally send those letters to you so that you may see how I've been. When you do hear from me, Tedward, please write in reply.

I love you.

~Jennifer.

Dear Tedward,

I know John didn't send the letter. I also know that in the event you read these letters; you might read them out of order. Last week's letter I touched on some issues I was having with the new church I attended. These teachings are false in every sense of the word, and I cannot stand to go to a place like this again. It's almost, no matter where I turn, I find a church to go to that is riddled with hatred and othering of others, and of course, isn't biblical. Every church has their short comings, and with the warming community, and there being peers of which we might relate to, we elected to give them the benefit of the doubt; however, they do not represent kindly the God whom I love.

As you can imagine, that is damaging to a church. Any community really. This has taken its toll on Samantha. In church last week, she had a PTSD episode, frozen up and screaming out in the middle of a sermon as she tried to leave, tripping over a few congregants in the process. Michael, Tim, and I went over to her to try to calm her down. The sermon all but stopped, and I could hear people in the church talking amongst themselves about Sam, presuming her to be demon possessed and among other things, spawn of the devil. There is nothing funny about this, that anyone would assume to know who she was.

So, we calmed her down, and I took her down to the fellowship hall, and into the bathroom away from the jeers. After calming her down, we took her out of the bathroom, and sought to find a way out without bringing too much attention, but she resisted, and I must say, though at the time, might have been considered a clever idea, she resisted and wanted to get a cup of coffee on the way out.

So, we did. What we experienced was awful.

They screamed at her on the way out. Wouldn't let her near the coffee machine, and usually, there was some kind of snack, usually a cake, and they wasted no time getting to them, and throwing the snack filled plates at her, calling her the devil, and some not so appropriate things that I dare not repeat, spoken or written. Enraged, justly, I think, I went over to the coffee table, and flipped it over, nearly hurting myself in the process.

I was so angry. I wanted to curse them. But I didn't. I forgave them in my heart, but even now, my blood still boils. This was as if there wasn't enough pain in the world to experience further discomfort within the sanctity of a Church. It could be expected. I don't think God was in that church. That's not His house. He is elsewhere, and we will find it.

I think it's fair to say, Tim, Michael, Sam nor I will never attend that church again. We thought we found the right one, but we were wrong. I hope God will forgive them because I'm finding it hard to do. It's difficult for me. We weren't seen. We weren't cared for. No one offered a hand, but we have each other, and we'll rely on that for the time being.

Michael had spent some time volunteering at a soup kitchen. He is helpful, always wanting to do more. Of course, John was there since it was unusual for Michael's day to day routine, watching should Michael say anything. I helped a little, and Sam was with Tim at home during this, processing the events I explained above. I helped a little, saw Michael's smile on his face, one of those was overdue since no honeymoon. Anyway, John helped me out of the soup kitchen. When he's not being a jerk, he can be polite and nice.

He walked me to a nearby park to rest my feet on the bench. We sat together. No. I swear. There isn't anything like that between us. To even think of such a notion. We talked for a little while. Asked how we were. You know, after what seems to be more than half a year, you'd think he'd ask that question more than just this one time! We're under house arrest essentially. We can't leave anywhere without him knowing or giving us the okay. If we leave, we need to go by his schedule. You know why. Anyway, I asked him about the letters there, and them being sent before I tried to mail the last one.

He told me some telling things which makes sense, but I didn't think to put the pieces together. But the one thing that doesn't make sense, is that it makes sense. An oxymoron if ever there was one. Try piecing that together. He said he saved it but didn't mail it. Put it with the rest of them. Well, at least he was honest this time. I asked him why he couldn't say why. And he gave me a cryptic answer.

He told me of a Pendragon. Uther, the first one, according to that ancient legend of which no historian can agree if was fact or fiction, and then subsequently, the birth of Arthur Pendragon. Arthur united the peoples of England against the celts and savages of the world before turning in on themselves, and reimagining a new rule of Kingdom where diplomacy reigned supreme. John told me in great length that the spirit of Pendragon was designed to be their own portion of God. Designated to them, and them alone. This portion was not as sufficient, as he said, as to that of my portion. He even complimented me, saying he'd prefer my portion over the one he received, and his was a mockery of what mine was. I asked him to elaborate on what he believed then, since he appeared to know more about God than I did, or so I thought so, but I don't exactly believe everything he told me. In fact, I don't really believe any of it. Besides the fact that the details of such belief are not meant for my ears. I wonder, perhaps, could you be a descendent of Arthur Pendragon?

That would be something, now wouldn't it? My Tedward, the descendent of a King. I sure know how to pick them, don't I?

But there was something that stuck out to me. While I may not believe the words he said, I do believe he understands his faith to be the right one. He said that now, his people are under a curse, caused by something that cannot be mended. And Hell, he put it, is the only place they can go, or else risk a state of nothingness. He admitted, his faith was the one true faith, and his people owned the truth. In more ways than one. But then he contradicted himself by saying my Faith was the correct one. I mean, of course it is, but why did he contradict himself? No matter, I'll try to ignore it. But if what he said happened to be true, what would your fate be?

After this conversation with John, I got home, and I went to bed. This week was like Hell. Do not recommend. But I also had a dream. No. A nightmare is best to describe this, and what I saw was so terrible, I can't begin to describe it. It's so horrible, I woke up screaming. I was looking at it from above, the things I saw.

I saw earth. In its glory with black clouds coalescing over it. Armies, and these creatures of what form they took, I do not know. Some were like Greek mythical creatures. And others from some places I do not know, but there were many. There were legions. Men fought against men, guns, steam ships, medieval weapons. People like Michael, Sam, Tim, and I were pitted against one another, and then there were those like John, and yourself, pitted likewise in such fashion. The beasts attacked all things living and devoured the dead.

The world had a heartbeat, and it beat loudly, thumping once, causing the ground beneath the crust to remove itself, pulsating like a human heart. Lava poured out of the cracks while everyone screamed until earth was consumed. The rest of the stars and the planets likewise were consumed, and I saw a brief glimpse of that beautiful flower before there was nothingness. I don't know what it means. I don't understand what context I was in, but it was clear that whatever that was, spoke unspeakable horrors to me. Perhaps I dreamt it because of what happened with the incident at my church. I don't know. Maybe you might make sense of it.

Anyway, that's all any updates I have. I love you, Tedward.

~Jennifer

Hey Ted,

It's me, Sam. So, I'm not sure why I'm even writing this. Jennifer asked me to, and I know John Spadero will not mail these letters, nor tell us where you are. But Jennifer wants me to write you a letter and send it to be mailed through John. SO, I personally find this useless as you'll never see it. Not when it matters. Why am I writing these letters instead of Jennifer?

This is my one and only letter, so I'll be quick about it, but make sure to get all the important pieces coming from me, and that which I imagine Jennifer wants to make sure you know. Well, the reason I'm writing this, is because of Jennifer, and for her as my love steeps into her heart as hers does mine, and Michael's and Tim's.

Jennifer hasn't been feeling well lately. She's been hiding it from us or so. I'll let her give you more details. I don't read these letters. So, I don't know what's in them, but I imagine she kept you informed on the day to day, telling you what's been going on with her week by week. Let me first talk about myself.

Ever since Boston. I still see the things, the blood, bones, soon, ash, corpses, and flies. I smell the flesh, the soot, and the flames, and I hear the exploding cars, the shards of glass, and the roar of cannon fire. It jolts me. I can't work right now because of it, and the triggers can be something small, or it can be big.

I find myself wondering how you did it? You see these things every night, hear them, smell, feel, see aging memories of your friends, no longer with us. Whether they are in Heaven or Hell, well, that's God's domain. I can't speak anything of it. How did you manage to keep yourself in check out in the public for so long, pretending everything was fine? I want to discipline myself to be more like you, so I'm not afraid of these things and that I can function without fear of being triggered out in the open, and risk being called a devil, a demon, or Satan's slut. Should we, no, we'll never meet again, but if we do, please teach me how you did it. I know it wasn't perfect, but at least for a time, you could function out in the real world as a real person. I cannot do that. I'm seeing a therapist, getting medication, not working, exercising, music therapy, and while it all seems to work for something, it doesn't take away the triggers that cause my episodes.

Well, that's off my chest, and we're all finally accepting that Erin and her mother's dead, and there was not, nor will there be a proper funeral for them. Just lumped together with the memorial they built out there. We can make phone calls to our families to touch base, but we can never go there. Michael and I are married, not sure if she told you that. It seems I lucked out, and he got the short end of the stick, having to put up with my attitude and periodic episodes.

Ted, I must switch gears now, and I know this is going to seem abrupt, and here I am, pretending you're going to read this letter before it really matters. Ted, this isn't going to be easy to hear. So, please, take some time before continuing to read this letter, and I'll continue writing while you go and have some time to sit down, relax, get a cup of coffee, or whatever it is you need to brace for something. Now, we don't know for certain what it is, I'll let Jennifer tell you the specifics.

Between Michael, Tim, and I, we believe she has more than just leukemia. Her condition took a turn, not for the worst, but it isn't great. She had another fall, and this time, she broke her wrist, had some serious bruising besides, and there was bleeding as to be expected. She's in the hospital now, and they're taking her in for some tests. She'll be there for a while, managing the tests, getting her already to go home. I think she'll be discharged by the end of the week. May we know the results of the test so we can see what exactly it is?

Anyway, Ted, take care of yourself.

I appear to be pulling a Jennifer, as if you will actually get the chance to read this. It's almost like you're actually still here.

~Samantha and Michael Harris.

Hi Tedward,

I know Sam sent the letter to John to be mailed. I just got out of the hospital, discharged. My wrist is in a cast. Sam, Michael, and Tim signed it. I'm not sure what they did for Church this week. They didn't say. Nor did they say anything about a Bible study of sorts, but I should indicate that I'm eager to get back into it, and I'm still waiting for the biopsy, and all the bloodwork to get back to me so I can see what all else is going on with my body.

I was in the hospital all week, so I don't really have much to say, I mean, "Ow." Tedward, if you can so help it, do whatever you can not to take a tumble down the steps as I did. Terrible business. Why would people do this?

Well, I've been in constant prayer anyway. Talking to God, praying the same prayer, feeling His presence within me.

I also was not able to look outside with an open window. Neighbors. Such dribble wouldn't allow me the pleasure. That's not true. I opened my window just a crack and all my neighbors complained because it was so cold. It's so warm down here I wouldn't even notice. So, trying to be a good neighbor, I elected to shut the window, and forego my own comfort until I returned safe in the bed in which Michael and Sam led me in.

Oh, we did go out for some ice cream. Vanilla, the unsung hero of all icy treats. Anyway Tedward, I cannot find much more to write about right now, the hospital had me under a spell. I'm sure I'll have more to write to you next week. Perhaps Sam can write you some more.

I love you.

~Jennifer.

Hi Tedward.

This letter isn't easy for me to write. Did Samantha write to you the letter I asked? Well, not sure if you'll get it anyway. It's been sometime since I've had the will to write a letter. I was discharged from the hospital and got the results from the prognosis. Even my mind is in a fog. A fog that clouds the words I want to say to you, to profess my feelings and my selfish desires plaguing my heart. Forgive me for being less than elegant in this letter, perhaps much later, I will find the strength to return to felicity, but a state of joy and happiness is out of my reach, and God, it feels has departed from me, or rather, my feeling of grief for this news that I've just received is preventing me from drawing near to His presence.

Tedward, I don't know how much longer I'm going to be able to keep these letters going. I've spoken with Tim, Sam, and Michael and they will support me with the new trial that I am facing. I cannot tell you if it is a good trial, or a just one. I know not if it comes from God, or as a result of my sin. I cannot tell you if I'm happy, for I am just filled with misery. I will keep on writing as long as I have energy. As long as God provides me the strength and inspiration to write these letters and profess my feelings towards you.

I love you, Tedward. No matter what happens, in this life or in life everlasting, I want you to know that I love you. You must know that you are forever loved by me. You asked me once, no. I'll not ponder on that now. But it's so hard to ponder anything else. I guess, there is no uncomplicated way to say this, not one bit. I've been putting it off for too long. Far too long.

The result of the test is that because of the waiting, because of the lack of a donor, and because of other things that are currently breaking down in my body, I have gone terminal. I don't want to die. They gave me six months. Provided I continue with the treatment plans. Of which are a bore, but I will take them, and follow through with the letter as I reflect on the closing chapter of my life, and my one regret, is that I can't spend it with you.

If I could have one thing; I want to spend my final days with you here, but I know that's a big ask. I know John could never and would never make such arrangements, and that despair is tearing at my heart. I'm dying, physically, and my mental and spiritual life is fading. I can feel it.

Michael and Samantha are wonderful and understanding with my current needs being what they are. We've already been talking about hospice care, and Samantha wants me with her during my last days, so that she knows I'm cared for. I will stay here. With her, with Michael, and periodically with Tim. I will try to continue to write, but even this letter is hard for me.

I know I am confident in my salvation with God, and it looks like I'll be seeing him face to face soon. And I know I should be joyous, but it means leaving you forever.

I know you asked me, 'what if I die' and when I answered, I never thought it would be so soon. At least, I didn't think so, didn't have cause to know, and didn't have cause to think anything of it, or to assume I'd go like this. I'm in pain, constantly filled with fatigue, and sometimes my legs feel like glass when I step on them. Moving forward as I do. I know I said wherever you go, my spirit will be with you, and I will be watching with a spare eye as often as I can, so that I may see you still. I pray, fervently, that whatever curse has befallen your people by ways and causes unknown, it can be uplifted.

I must go. I need to take some time away. I'll write again, I just don't know when. Could be next week. Could be next month. I don't know.

Tedward. Know that I love you.
~Jennifer

Hey Ted,

I guess I should start writing you letters of which I know you'll never receive. I find it oddly therapeutic. I guess I know why Jennifer does it so much. Anyway, it's taking me some time to process. Jennifer is dying. I think she said we have six months left with her. It's tragedy after tragedy, and I'm beginning to feel a sense of helplessness as we go through this. Memories are fading with me. We are helpless and hopeless during these trying times. I was unable to save Erin. She died in front of me. I was unable to do anything regarding Emily. I couldn't do anything as the church called me the devil's slut. And now, I can't do anything now that Jennifer's dying, and she's going to pass from this world.

I see, through a fog. Although, I somehow always knew it to be the case, knowing is one thing. Experiencing it is another. This world is filled with so much cruelty, and I just want to give up. My health and mental health, while stable, is still deteriorating. I feel like a thousand needles pricking apart my brain, steeping me lower into insanity, and Jennifer was the one who pulled me out of it, kept pulling me out of it, and now it seems I'm to be to Jennifer what she was to me, only I haven't improved. Michael and Tim are the only sane ones left, and for how long until they start losing it. Tim is taking this especially hard. He loved her, just as she loved you. A weird triangle if ever there was one. And it was barely there. Jennifer and you, a love that would and could never be.

But she was so good for you. She was so good to you. She understood what you were, who you were, and knew that you were deprived of some knowledge, and prepared you for that. Who would ever think that such a detail as washing apples would mean and tell us so much about you? She's weeping in the other room right now. We don't know exactly what the next six months are going to be like, but we're there for each other.

I want to see you Ted, talk to you about the things I've been personally experiencing. But I know more than anything else, Jennifer needs you more than anyone else. The church has for some reason, seemed to abandon us, and Michael and Jennifer didn't appreciate it that much. Those two, they're almost too pure for a world as cruel as this. She wants to spend the rest of her days with you.

Can I make this happen? I doubt it. John Spadero will not even mail these letters. I doubt he'll make an exception and get you a plane ticket here, a hotel just for you to stay. You know what? I don't care. I don't care about the hotel. You can stay here. Ted, if I can make this happen, will you show up? I hope to God and all that is left to be good in this world that your answer is yes, and I hope eagerly that you will accept the invitation in the moment it becomes feasible.

I'll talk to John and keep you updated.

I swear, I'm beginning to sound like Jennifer, as if you'll ever see this letter.

~Samantha Harris.

Dear Tedward,

It turns out God gave me the energy to write to you again this week. My condition hasn't improved. I don't expect it to, it'll only get worse, and my bones will become increasingly brittle throughout the next several months before, what shall not be named come to pass. It's still hard, trying to accept it, but the sooner I come to terms with it, the better. We're waiting on some supplies, gauze, bandages, and the like since I'm more prone to bleeding than I was before, and sometimes, a crack in the skin is all it takes.

I had to take some time away from work, and I quit. I loved the job, but if it means shortening my life for not taking proper care of myself, I'd rather not work. It's not like it did much financially to begin with, and I have Michael and Sam to help look after me. They encouraged me to quit my job while they could make up for the extra work in other ways to help provide for themselves, and me. Michael stopped working the soup kitchen temporarily, at least until, well, you know.

I spoke with my parents the other day, and they're heartbroken about it. They'll be coming down to visit. It's hard, you know, them asking why I can't come and visit them. Reason one, I shouldn't be leaving Sam's house much anyway. Secondly, the agreement. I hate that agreement. It keeps us apart, it keeps me isolated; it keeps us all isolated. I don't like that.

I had another dream, Tedward. The world was cracked open, filled with blackness. Convoluted in a black fog, and on it, appeared the cracks gaze way through the gates of hell, while a legion, no, it was a modest group of people clothed in those colorful veins of yours leaving into a giant cup, and disappeared into the great beyond. Where did they go? I wonder. What was left of the world was little more than husks, dead bodies being devoured by the same creatures I saw in the previous Hellish nightmare I had. In this dream, there was no screaming for the screams of agony were already complete.

I know these letters aren't nearly as long as my previous ones, not even half a page. But I cannot muster up the strength to keep going. Until next time, then?

I love you.

~Jennifer.

Hey Ted,

So, we invited Jennifer's family over from New York. They'll be visiting town for a couple of weeks before they get back. We don't want to start making specific arrangements for the inevitable just yet, as everyone is still in shock. Suddenly, this happened, but with hindsight bias, we should have expected this was going to be the result. We didn't push hard enough. No. I keep wanting to blame myself for this, feeling like there is always a solution if I just pushed hard enough. But unfortunately, sometimes there isn't a solution, and I too must come to terms with that. Michael is urging Jennifer to speak to a lawyer to put a will together.

He stopped barking up that tree when she said she didn't have anything worth giving to anyone. Journals maybe, but she was saving them for something special.

I asked her if she wanted anything, and she asked for a photograph journal. We bought one, it was hefty. I don't know what she wants to fill in it, but she asked us to take photographs of all the places we were in, all the people we've seen, and many of us, around the dinner table having community with one another, processing the pictures at a processing center, and then sticking them into the book. She was very eager about this. I don't know what she intends to do with it. It makes her happy, and she needs to be happy, so let her be. We also got her a little journal, and she writes in it every day. I think she treats it like a prayer journal.

So, I gave John the two letters. One from me, the other from Jennifer. I told him what was going on with Jennifer, and he was broken up about it. He cried in his office. It makes me sick, honestly, given all the shit he's put us through. Why? He barely knows us personally, and he holds our shackles. What cause did he have to cry? Forgive my language. Anyway, I tried to push him for getting you here. He declined, said, policy for the agreement. That damned agreement can rip itself to shreds and go to Hell. As you can imagine, I didn't get anywhere with him this week.

But this week is going to be different. How you ask? Simple. I'm going there every day until he caves and makes the call to wherever you are to make arrangements to get you here. Jennifer wants to see you, and I want to make that happen. She deserves better than what John will allow her to have.

Anyway, even you deserve better than what you received. I'm talking via letters in a world of tragedy, and as if you were the punch line to some cruel joke, tossed to and from like a ragdoll thrust into the wind. A cliché, I know, but it fits you just as well. I wish we could pull you out of that darkness more fully, so that you don't have to remember the past you were forced into.

Well, I must be going. I've got to get things prepared for dinner tonight. I'll let you know how I do next week.

Sincerely,
Sam Harris

Hey Ted,

It's me, Sam again. Well, these letters are therapeutic. Well, I'll get right to the point. I spoke with John every day this week, pushing for him to do it. I'm sure if he didn't have to keep an eye on us, he'd have screened my calls, and forced them to voicemail. So, I've got that to my advantage as I walk into his office every day, regardless of whether or not he had a meeting to attend to, important or otherwise. I may have become a thorn in his side. Serves him right for not doing something so simple, and not mailing all these letters we keep sending him. It really isn't that hard.

But again, another wall. I couldn't get him to budge, and on Friday, it's Sunday now, And I spoke with his assistant later that evening and asked me about my concerns with Ted. I told her everything. I'm surprised she didn't know already, I guess John keeps her in the dark with certain things as much as he keeps the rest of the world in the fog. Anyway, I asked for her help, and she said she will pester him at night.

Which means, he'll hear this request every single day until he agrees. Until he arranges a flight, and until I ensure it will factually happen. I worked in logistics. I know how to check my freight!

Anyway, talk to you soon.

~Samantha Harris

Good morning Tedward,

I know it's been a few weeks, but I took a slight dip. Energy has been nonexistent as of late. I've been working on something, and I hope, should you ever see it, well, I hope you'll see it. I must say, I'm proud of it, I hope you'll be proud of it too. I've been working on it for a bit. I'll not tell you what it is, I want it to be a surprise.

My family arrived this week. They flew in, they stayed at a nearby hotel, since Sam and Michael couldn't accommodate them on such short notice, except for food, and whatnot. We talked a lot, and of course we were all very hush hush on the "agreement" thing, and they pressed no further on that. We played some games, and had lots of fun, and of course, I spoke about you to my parents. They asked me some pressing questions, as I tend to overromanticize everything. Little Jane Austen in me. They even asked me when they'll meet you, as if they were still optimistic about my condition.

We don't need to talk too much about that, but they were very thankful for Michael and Sam's hospitality. I just realized something. The word "Hospital" is in the word, "Hospitality." I don't like that word anymore I decided. I need a new one. I'll have to get back to you on that one.

Sam is up to something. I don't know what. She's been gone for some time, coming to and fro, swiftly exiting upon arrival to go somewhere. I asked her where she was going, as I wanted to spend time with her earlier this afternoon, and then she left just as quickly as she arrived. She told me, she can't tell me, but that it was for me. I, of course, shrugged. But who could blame her?

Okay, I need to cut this line short as I'm about to get depressed. I feel a dark spirit looming over me. Until next time.

I love you.
~Jennifer.

Ted.

Thank God! That man has a limit, and we've broken him. We broke the man into doing it, and my skills as a broker and aggression was required, so please forgive me for whatever John may decide to do to me and to you because of it. I can tell you greatly, the weight of this burden is now lighter. And I can breathe easily. Thank God.

When I left the office today, I could kiss the ground, if it wasn't chronically littered with dog poop. I don't even know where to begin. It took a while. It's been a good long while actually. Thankful! Thankful! Thankful! And of course, it wouldn't have been possible without his assistant.

Wait.

Look at me getting so excited. Not everything's finalized with this just yet. So, here's how Friday went, I came in at my usual time, and I swear, the security might think John is up to something. He is always up to something, but no one could ever know. But when I came in, he started shouting at me in irritation. His assistant was there, pestering him likewise, and with the sudden noise, I guess security was about to come in.

They knocked on the door asking if everyone was all right, and I may have gone a little overboard and would have said something along the lines of, oh, you know, what would happen if I told them everything. Every detail. John fumed and his face turned red with a fit of rage. Unable to think about putting out that fire, he agreed to call his boss (whoever that was) tomorrow. I said, no.

That wasn't good enough. Call him right now! And so, he complained about it being late, no way is his boss who knows who you are, is going to pick up the phone. Suggesting some kind of time zone, so, now I know you are somewhere else. Europe. Asia, Australia, or Africa: so many places to choose from. I urged him; we would not leave him alone unless he placed the call.

So, he did. He spoke with someone on the phone regarding the predicament and mentioned you by name as the name we knew you by. He went on paced back and forth, and finally John gave the phone to me, and I took it eagerly. The man on the other line was gentle, but he did note that we should be thankful that they chose to leave us alive and should be thankful for that much.

His name was Adam Sander. We spoke for a good long while. John let me have the room for some reason. So, I took advantage of it and sat in his chair. Those chairs are comfy. Anyway, I told him everything, this Adam fellow, and he seemed to be empathetic on the phone to our plight, and I said to him, and urged him, that you and I have a mutual friend who is dying. And that her last wish was to see him in person before her passing. He asked how long she was expected to live under her condition, and I told him about six months.

He didn't want to budge, but he said this, that the answer is 'maybe' right now. He needs to make a few phone calls and make arrangements. He took down my contact information and I need not bore you with the details. That's funny. You won't see this letter. John won't freaking mail them! But anyway, I have a virtual appointment with him next Friday, about the same time. It'll be between me, him, and someone by the name of Bridgette. And there, I guess we'll discuss details on releasing you over to us for a few months, at least until, well, the end.

Hey.

I want you to know that you're still part of this little dysfunctional family, and no, Jennifer didn't put those words here, I did. Can you not tell with my handwriting? If we're allowed to talk or visit after, or you are, I want you to know our door, Michael, and Mine, are always open to you. I don't care if you come knocking at 3:00 AM. You knock, and the door will be open to you. Always.

We love you. We all do. Me. Jennifer. And Michael. Maybe not Tim since he doesn't know you too well, but I'm sure he'll still be happy to see you. Well, wish me luck, and let's pray that the meeting goes just as smoothly as possible.

~Sam

Good morning Tedward,

I was able to take a walk today. I couldn't go too far now, since I need to stay relatively close to the house. Perhaps if I wasn't too paranoid, but I'd rather not be too uncomfortable, and if I can afford to forego some trips to the hospital and emergency room, I'd much rather do that, and be a little more comfortable, feel the wind, the grass prickle against my skin. I look forward to the day where I can feel my new body. Of course, that might not mean anything to you, but maybe I'll describe it much later. It can be a very convoluted topic.

Today was a good day, more or less, really. Some things. I attempted to draw. I can't draw. Not a steady hand, so unfortunately, I'll not be making any wondrous illustrations. Not that I could ever draw before, thought I'd try my hand at it. Not for me. I'll get back into reading another book.

It's been a good day for me physically, but emotionally I've felt just a tad bit isolated. Not from Michael, or Samantha, though, she did spend a lot of time with me this week. More than last week. She seemed incredibly happy, like she accomplished something. I know not what of course. She did say it was for me. I wonder what could be so secretive. I don't know if she even told Michael or not. Anyway, I feel like much more is coming, and I can sense God's presence here, but I feel isolated not going to Church. Michael and Sam have stopped trying to find one altogether. I asked them why, and they said that they don't think there's a church suitable for them, or me.

Goodness gracious. Sam had one outburst and was labeled as the devil. I can only imagine what a church might say about me. They might turn me into Job. Oh, I have some sin I haven't repented for. Or God is doing this to me because of some relapsed sin of my parents. I mean, what? I'm confident I know my Bible better than they do, and certainly what they're suggesting is straight up heresy. Treating me like

I have leprosy or some other plague of equal contagion. It's not contagious. And neither is PTSD, but they treat it like it is. People are so undereducated here.

We've kind of made our own little Church here, and we fellowship closely with one another on Sundays. Tim is also involved as he's the only one of us who has any gift of singing. Sam's getting quite good at the violin though. She's making it sing harmoniously. And it fills the room, and you can almost feel a warmth, though the world may be dark, and the world may be cold, in that space, in that room during that time, it's filled with light, and warmth, and so much if it, it's very cozy.

I'm tired. I think I'm going to turn in for the night. Good night Tedward.

I love you.

~Jennifer

Hey Ted,

This letter is coming late. I do wonder if John reconsidered and is now sending these letters. Unbelievably, I missed an opportunity and forgot to ask Adam if John could send the letters. I supposed I won't have another chance to ask them about the letters, but you know what, that doesn't even matter anymore. I suppose I can ask John about this, and he might say, sure, I'll take it. Or why are you bothering me with this again? Maybe I just feel the urge right now to write pointless letters, waste the stampage and send it to John out of habit now.

Well, I just had that meeting, and a decision has not yet been made as to whether or not Adam will release you. It felt very much like an interview. Who we are, what we want with you, regardless that I told them exactly that. But when most people say they're trying to know who we are, often they refer to our own identity. I think they were looking more at my character as a person before contemplating further negotiations. They spoke at length with themselves muted on my screen, but they talked with one another, him, and Bridgette. They were beside themselves, and both of them.

I saw them both. And both of them looked too familiar, but not the type of familiarity of which one associates with friends, family, or a long-lost friend. They like you, Ted. Their eyes. Bags underneath them as they too struggled with sleep, and they too saw despair and were perpetually depressed. They were you, Ted. They are you. I must have been too caught up when I saw Culain, Ilya, Alex, and Blanka to see the same, but they were there. The bags in their eyes. All the time. Reflecting on it now, I see it in John's eyes, and now too. I was too naïve to see it in John, but I see it now. You two, you all are suffering the very same thing: isolation and loneliness with a burden heavier than a mountain.

I'm so sorry. I didn't do any of this to you all. Nor did you ask for any of this, but this, whatever this is, is causing you all so much pain, and the world we live in is just so cruel to watch you all unfold into tragedy. I'm sorry, for the pain that you all feel. And I'm especially sorry there isn't any tangible way for me to fix this world. But pray. And pray I will.

This is already becoming a long-winded letter, and I'm already weeping. I've wiped my eyes a few times already since penning this letter down. I must get to the point. So, they didn't decide. They will continue with another round of meetings, and they advised I should hear from John what the decision will be, and that I must respect the decision. I told them, the only way I will accept that decision, is if the answer is, when can I pick you up from the airport. I told them they were fools if I'd accept anything less than that. Those were my terms. And I told them if they genuinely cared for your wellbeing and wishes, that they would consult you before they even entertain the idea of denying this request. I'm sure you yourself want to be here with us, with Jennifer during her last days. I said I was going to make it happen. I'm going to make it happen. So just hang in there, a little while longer. I should hear something before next Friday. So, with that, I guess I'll talk to you then.

I suppose I should start thinking of something, for us all to do for this reunion. Maybe I'm getting my hopes up, but I'll make a way. Rather, God will make a way when there is none. He will open this door, and I am but a tool. I've shattered your steel trap; I can shatter this. If it's the last thing I do. Well, now, I think myself a fool. You can't respond to this. I guess, like Jennifer, I found myself lost in the art of writing a letter I've forgotten that one, you can't see this now, and are unlikely to see it soon. How silly of me. Perhaps John will mail them, perhaps not, and we can collect the letters and send them back off with you when you return back to where they call you to be.

Goodbye Ted.

We love you.

Sam and Michael Harris.

Dear Mrs. Samantha Harris,

Rerouted through the office of Mr. John Spadero.

With careful consideration upon your request regarding a Mr. Ted Anderson, and his personal leave from his duties from the 'Administration,' prolonged per abnormal circumstances, the 'Administration' is pleased to inform you that your request has been authorized, but activity will be heavily supervised. Ted Anderson, along with Bridgette Smith, will be departing Friday September 17th, 5:00 AA EST and will be arriving approximately 1:25PM EST at the RRW international airport.

Arrangements have already been made for lodging for both Ted Anderson and Bridgette Smith and no further action will be required on your part. His return is contingent upon his own request, or Bridgette's. There are no hospitality requirements for Bridgette while she is in company.

Note: It is required that Bridgette accompany Anderson at all times.

TED!

It's Sam. I know, not the usual greeting. I just opened the mail today and received a letter from a Mr. John Spadero. I know, not the one you were hoping for. So, I opened it, and I received a bunch of papers inside, and I must say, that man will do what he must, but when it comes from the top, he does it and performs as the letter dictates for him to do. I know not what his intentions were for the rest of the letters we sent.

It only took three weeks.

I really hope they got you ready. I have a spare room for you when you arrive. I see the itinerary, and I'm picking you up from the airport. I'll get a room ready, and of course, I must tell Jennifer. I should be subtle about it, she's bound to have a heart attack, though the added excitement will be good for her, I think. She's still off and on, some days are clearly better than others, and some days it gets worse. We've done what we can, researched some diets for her to try to see if it helps at least.

She's gone full vegetarian, and so have our meals. Michael misses his chicken, and he will occasionally go out just to get some chicken for himself. I don't really care for meat too much, so it didn't bother me. Took some time trying to get used to it anyway. I don't know. I'll roll with it. Whatever it is. We'll be driving a green SUV when we pick you up. We'll have Jennifer with us, so she can be excited to see you off the plane.

You know what? Screw it. No. She's getting a surprise. I'll pick you up in our car. I'll be texting Michael so he can prepare her for something. I'll tell her there's a surprise coming, but she won't know what it is. We'll do this all secret like so no one will ever know but Michael and I, and Sakura I'm sure knowing. I have to find her and tell her not to say anything to Jennifer about it. Not that they talk.

I don't need to include more into this.

I will SEE you next week. I'm going to hug you; I hope you don't mind. You don't have a choice. I'm hugging you. We'll catch up.

Love Michael, Sam, Tim, and Jennifer.

Dear Tedward,

I must say, I had another dream. It felt peaceful, and serene, like perfection, as if I stared right into the garden of Eden itself. My legs were no longer glass, and I was walking without shoes, and the ripples of the lake flowed around me, my feet causing the waves to approach the ends of it. The water was cool, and the air, warm as it caressed my skin, and my bones, with each step, walked carefully, but they weren't brittle, and they didn't feel like glass, and my weight wasn't going to shatter them, nor give me cause to fall.

I stared out over the horizon, the orange hue of the light descending upon a hill, and a silhouette of a person standing over the hill, walking, no, wobbling down the hill. It became clearer as I got to the shore, walking on the water, and I knelt down as the silhouette became clear, shadow faded, and the boy took his hand to the pond to drink. So too, did I drink the water, and it was clear, clean, water, of the most refreshing kind.

I looked into the eyes of the boy, and he at me. He had a wide smile, brimming almost ear to ear, with beautifully white teeth. His face was without blemishes, or scars, and his black hair neatly combed to both sides. His eyes also, didn't have bags underneath them, nor were they filled with exhaustion. He was utterly filled with supreme felicity.

I took his hands in mine and studied them. Soft. Without callouses. No scars, and the water kept them clean. And I took my hands to his face, rubbing his cheeks. Don't ask me why. I don't know, and I saw deeply into the soul of this boy, and he reminded me of you. Is this what you would have been like had the unspeakable not happened to you? Would you have been filled with so much joy to have it carelessly stolen away? Well, I mustn't think too much on the matter. We can't change the past by reflecting upon it, but we could change the future if we tried.

Promise me something, should you ever read this letter. You are a man of influence, and you are far from stupid. Childish sometimes, maybe, bitter, but neither are you a fool, nor do you think hotheaded. You can change the world, and it would please me, if you could make a world without war, without violence, and without hate. I know that I am asking a lot, for it also means circumcising the hate already embedded in your heart. And that such a world, maybe, would ask that you be not in it. But I would implore you to do what you do best and kill the spirit of hatred within you, so that you may live the best life and give yourself the chance at the best possible life this world can offer. I know it can't offer much that will offset what it already took from you but something is better than nothing.

Well, enough of the fatalism of life. Let's talk about something a little happy. Samantha brought me flowers the other day, and a whole bouquet of flowers of various kinds. I'm not sure who helped her pick them out, but they were the most beautifully fragrant selection, and it uplifted my spirits. I have them sitting in a vase by my window, and I like to smell them before I go to bed. Flowers. I've never been particularly good with them, but they have a nasty habit of dying too quickly. Well, before I feel like their time should be up. I asked her what the occasion was, and she said, she has a surprise for me. Oh, joy! Whatever could it be! I don't know. I want the surprise. She said I'd really enjoy it, whatever it was. She didn't give me any more information than that, but she's never led me wrong before.

Anyway, I'll write to you next week. Let me see if I can break my silence of finding something more meaningful to talk about. I can always talk to you about my dreams if you'd like.

I love you.

~Jennifer.

Good morning Tedward,

Or whatever time of day your eyes happen to be on the ink of this page.

Well, if you're reading this, I've passed on and in my Father's arms, the Lord's arms.

I've been contemplating these words for a while, and words are like rudders of a ship, so small, yet such impactful. I don't want to say the wrong thing, and I don't want to come off as sad, and yet, I imagine you're probably crying over the pages right now. I can feel your warm tears on me, and I can feel your love pouring out over me. Just know, death wasn't the way it was supposed to end for us, but it did. And I'm no longer in pain. I'm not sad. I'm with my friends and family now, who are also with the Lord.

Please read my words carefully. I want you to know these things, and I want you to accept what I tell you as truth and not mere speculation. I know abundantly more about your curse than I did, for these things, God revealed to me in my dreams. Our spirits will never be one, and neither will our flesh, for you have a different path, a different destiny born under this curse. But your curse is going to be lifted. When you read the rest of the letters saved for you in this box. I spoke of a boy. That boy has been revealed to me, he's you. As you should be, and as you will become.

God has a plan for you and your people, but they are forever separated. You will be given a new home, a new earth to call your own and cultivate it with new and reformed bodies and spirits where negativity will die, hatred and despair will be nothing but myths. Your own little slice of heaven. Keep on running that race Tedward. Run, and find the light, I implore you! Find what little light is left in this world and hold on to it!

These last several months, that you and I have been together was what I needed to truly pass peacefully. I never thought I'd ever see you again, and be happy, and to think with so much time that passed between us, I am thankful that we continued where we left off. I'm so proud to have been part of your life, and to have you as part of mine. I am thankful for the gifts, the dancing, and the special chair you got me, just so that I could walk a little more comfortably with you as we went by. Thank you for being gentle with me in my aching body and being with me in my room at night.

I do appreciate Bridgette for being there and please pass this along to her. That she likewise is loved. I know it was impossible. But had it been, and had this been an option on the table, I would have loved to spend the rest of my life with you. But then, I guess I already did. Though she was present, she never once got in the way of us being together. Us housing with Sam and Michael, I felt like we were all united again, like one, big happy, dysfunctional human family. Before all this happened.

Now, I must close this off now. Even in death, I will always love you. Live the life you want to live that would be pleasing to me. My spirit will watch over you. I will be there to guide you to make the right choices so that you have a future to look forward to.

Enclosed within this letter is an envelope. It has Sam's name on it. I wanted you to hand it to her. For I want these words to have touched your hands so that they may touch her ears. Now, I think I remember saying I was working on something special to you. I want you to take care of it. Sam has it, hence why I need you to give her that letter.

This is Goodbye, Tedward. Know that I love you.

God's grace and peace be with you.

I love you.

With adoration that can only come through Christ, I love you.

~Jennifer.

Hey Sam,

Thank you for being a friend to me, and a friend to Ted, a friend to all as you were. Everyone needs a Sam. No one should go into their life without knowing a Sam, especially one that is as thoughtful, caring, and compassionate as you are. Yes, yes, I saw everything you did. And if anyone says they have the best friend in the world, and that world isn't you, well, clearly, they haven't met you, or they lied to everyone. You are the definition of a friend. And no friend could have anyone better than you. Michael really hit the jackpot when he asked for your last name.

Thank you. For being a part of my life and allowing me to be a part of yours. I love you, and Michael equally, and with such a passion that can pale only in comparison to the love of Christ. May He guide you and Michael in this world and bless your days with bliss and felicity. Be like Mr. Darcy and Ms. Bennet. I think finding the two out in the real world would be magnificent.

I thank you. For staying with me in my final days and final hours and providing for my needs as I struggled. Thank you for being there during my final hour, and I can't thank you enough for what you did for me. That's why you are not just a friend, you are the friend of friends, and one friend that stands out from the crowd, where someone who knows and reads of your exploits of the friend supreme will point to you and say, "That is the friend I want to be." I had a problem. The problem with an impossible wall and red tape to cut through, layers on layers, but that didn't stop you. You cut off that tape! You broke down that wall with the same level of tact the Apostle Paul had. Subtle as a jackhammer on a Sunday morning.

You brought Ted back to me. And me back to him. That was my one final wish. Though I only just wanted to see him one last time, but that wasn't enough for you. You brought him back, so that I may spend the rest of my life with him, as short as it was. Sounds like the plot of some weird romantic novel that ends in tragedy. Well, anyone expecting a happily ever after will undoubtedly be disappointed. But I am not.

I have a safe, in my room. Ted bought it for me. Combination is 6-13-22. Can you open it? There's a photo album I've been saving. I have two of them. One is larger than the other. That one is for you and Michael. It has memories of me and us all over the last year. The other is specifically for Ted. Please give it to him. Tell him these are pictures of the two of us and all our adventures together. While we were here. I want him to have a memory of me, and him, and you all. Yes, you, Michael, and Tim are included in the photos inside his album.

Sam. Just as you were a friend to me. So also, be a friend to Ted. He needs it. Now, more than every with me is gone. Be there for him. You and Michael. Please. This light is dark, you know that. His heart is dark. Be the light to contrast his darkness. Be there for him. I'll say hi to Erin for you, Tim, and Michael.

I am filled with the love of God as I go into His arms. I am filled with the joy of knowing you all, and while I am content, I would be lying if I said I wasn't scared. I love you. This is goodbye.

Sam. My dear Sam. I love you.

I look forward to seeing you all on the other side.

Until we meet again.

Goodbye.

~Jennifer

Jennifer Jane Anderson(31) was born on August 12th in Buffalo, NY 1989 and passed away March 13th, 2016, Washington DC. She most recently lived with her best friends Michael and Samantha Harris. She moved to DC in the early spring of 2025. She is survived by Shawn (Father) and Rachel (Mother) Miller, John (Brother) Miller, and Ted Anderson (Husband).

Acknowledgements.

My grandparents who have urged me to continue writing and fostered my imagination from a young age. The Paper tiger for putting up with my shenanigans throughout our daily writing sprints, and of course, who could forget the talented Aimee Hill, for putting up with my weird concepts, of course, this is quite possibly the most normal thing I've written.

If you've followed me this far, thank you. I am most active on my twitter, but do have a newsletter on Substack if you'd like to stay in touch.

Twitter: @Sarcastic_elf

Substack: Armanis Ar-feinial

Armanis Ar-feinial, in the gritty pits of despair, he comes from: Bridgeton, Maine, a terribly dreadful place. Currently residing in the Greater Boston Area with his family, he studied Criminal Justice, English, and currently dabbles in a little bit of Finance. His unfaltering passion for writing came from his first exposure from the Lord of the Rings, which he drew inspiration from in his first stories, but alas, as all good things come downward into the grimdark pits, adopting tones from Joe Abercrombie. He loves reading, playing games of all kinds, and he is what you call a practicing writaholic. He is personally known for his witty sarcastic unasked for remarks.

www.ingramcontent.com/pod-product-compliance
Lightning Source LLC
Chambersburg PA
CBHW040835010826
48978CB00012BB/771